Lemons on Venus
And Other Stories

By Brad Glenn
Cover Photography by Gaelan Glenn

For Sarah and Ella

Table of Contents

After Momma Died Carrying The
Jelly Baby

After Momma died carrying the Jelly Baby, Poppa and Leon started acting strange. Poppa locked the door of his bedroom for two days, taking with him only a bottle of rye whiskey and a pail of peas Momma picked three days earlier. He finally came out to empty the bucket he used as a toilet, and then went into town for the next couple of nights, sleeping at the hotel and leaving me alone with Leon. Poppa ran from the house in such a hurry that he left his false teeth behind. They floated in a glass in the bathroom like the frogs in formaldehyde we dissected in science class.

Leon was the strongest of our family, holding the anxiety of Momma's death in like a breath. Leon was two years older than me, so he took on Momma's chores. I think Poppa wanted me to do it, being as I was suddenly the only female left in the house, but Leon took over her role without having to be asked. Leon was sixteen, and he had already dropped out of high school. He had been planning to work on the railway, but then Momma told him she was pregnant again. He was probably thinking that he was going to help her take care of the new baby, or maybe he thought it was a good excuse to stay home and not have to work, but either way, he did finally end up with the responsibilities of the household.

I never went to Momma's funeral. I didn't want to see her in that box, or get put into the ground. I heard my father's sisters in the spare room whispering 'she was too old for another child,' and 'he should be ashamed for making her go through with it.' I didn't want to hear those whispers while they buried her.

When my father called me to go, I hid behind the barn. After the car drove out of the yard, I walked to the swamp and sat.

That was when I saw him for the first time.

"So you couldn't go to the funeral, eh?" the voice spoke to me. "That's not very brave of you, Maggie."

"Who is it?" I called. The swamp burbled and spat, but I didn't see anybody.

"You don't recognize your own brother?"

"L...Leon?"

"No, he went. It's me, the Jelly Baby."

I looked down, and he was near my feet. I jumped back in fear. He was nearly transparent, except for the veins running blue and red down his body, making him look like a plastic bag filled with viscous fluid and coloured wool. He had an enlarged head and small, underdeveloped hands. His eyes were covered in a white film, and his mouth was wide, with tiny sharp teeth.
"Wait!" he called. I couldn't. I ran back to the house and locked myself inside. Hours later my father came home alone. Leon went to the after-funeral dinner, but my father was too worn out. He just sat in his Laz-E-Boy chair and watched television. I never told him about the Jelly Baby.

               *   *   *

"Jelly Baby?" I called, hoping not to get a response. It was around noon, and I felt relatively safe by the swamp.

"Maggie," he whispered in his gurgling, throaty voice. He was leaning up against a rock. "I didn't think you'd be back."

"Who are you?"

"I told you. I am your brother."

"But what are you doing here? You were never born. Didn't they bury you?"

"They were going to, but I escaped. They wanted to kill me, Maggie, and I'm not ready to die."

"How do you survive out here? I mean, it gets cold at night, and there isn't anything to eat."

"The swamp is warm, and there are so many frogs here that I only need to open my mouth and one will jump in. This is heaven."

"I want to talk about Momma."

"I thought you would," he said, rubbing his forehead with the slimy finger-stubs of his hand. He grinned, exposing his fine teeth.

"Did you kill her?"

"Yes, Maggie, I did." When he said this I breathed in hard, making my lungs hurt for a moment. He kept staring at me, serious.

"Why?"

"Everything dies, Maggie. Momma did, Poppa will. We are constantly in the process of death, and everything both has a creator and a destroyer. Your Grandmother was your Momma's creator, and I was her destroyer."

"But why now?" I asked. Jelly Baby shifted his weight, and I could see organs and arteries move around inside of his body.

"It was the proper time. I will die too, and soon."

"How soon?"

"Soon." I looked down at his pitiful body, and for a moment I almost thought of him as a brother, instead of a monster. Part of me wanted him to die, just to be rid of him, but some other part, some hidden side, was begging me to hold onto him, if only for a little longer.

*   *   *

I came home from school and Leon had a grilled cheese sandwich ready for me. I really didn't need him to make me one. I had been using the stove for three years by myself, and before then Momma had shown me how to make muffins and pies in the oven.

"Thanks for the sandwich, Leon."

"You're welcome, dear," he said, his voice was deep and strong. He had never called me dear before, and I got worried. As I walked to my room, I saw Leon bending over, throwing something into the trash. His pants rode up over his muscular ankle for a second, and I noticed hair pressed tight against his legs from Momma's nylons, but I couldn't understand why he was wearing them. I didn't say anything, and I don't think Poppa knew.

Poppa got home from his first day of work after Momma's death. He looked much better than he had for the previous month. His hair was combed, he had shaved, and he was wearing his teeth. He had a strange smile.

"Hi Poppa, how was work?"

"Everyone treated me like I had a disease. Like being a widower was contagious. I liked having everyone keep an arms distance from me, smiling through nervousness. No one came to me with problems, they just tried to work them out on their own. I like being intimidating."

*   *   *

Jelly Baby came to my room that night. I heard something softly thumping against the window, so I opened my curtains to see him leaning against it, like some great insect on a windshield. I opened it carefully, and he came inside. He asked for a bucket to sleep in, so I went to the garage and got one. It was clean, and only had some paint stains on the outside. I filled it with warm water and Jelly Baby pulled himself inside. I didn't touch the Jelly Baby.

"You haven't visited me lately. It's been over a week."

"No, I was busy."

"Too busy for your own brother? I understand. At times like this you need to think of yourself."

"I missed you."

"Really? You say it as though it were obligatory. You don't have to miss me, you know, not now anyway. Maybe tomorrow when I'm dead."

"What?"

"I've decided to die."

"What do you mean? You can't die."

"Yes I can, you can watch me if you don't believe it. I told you, everything dies." Then he rolled over in the water, staring up at me. He looked like a deformed cherub.

"How are you going to die?" I said. I was starting to cry, although I couldn't understand why. I barely even knew the Jelly Baby, and I didn't like him. I resented him.

"It isn't hard."

*   *   *

My digital alarm clock started playing music at four in the morning. I woke up and turned it off. Jelly Baby was on my bed, staring at me.

"Wha... What's happening?" I groaned, rubbing my eyes.

"I had to get you up. I set your alarm to go off."

"Why?"

"I'm leaving now. I want you to take me out to the swamp, where I'll die and leave you alone."

I sat up in bed, and looked at him.

"No, I won't!"

"You don't have a choice."

"I won't let you go!"

"You will," he said, and I looked at him. He seemed more fragile than before, more sad. He stared out at me through his milky eyelids, and for a moment I could understand the pain he felt.

Every nerve was exposed to the world, with no skin to protect him. I could make out the hollows of his translucent skull, and the movement of his pliable bones. "Please."

I got out of my bed, and sneaked the bucket to the front door. I put on my running shoes and walked out into the night air and to the swamp. Jelly Baby watched my face the entire time, never moving his glance to the sky or the ground.

"Empty me into the swamp, and I'll be gone," he said. I leaned over him, into the bucket, and kissed him on his forehead. It felt soft, a little like a peeled grape, and beautiful. He pulled his mouth back into a smile, and I dripped tears onto him.

"I love you," I whispered.

"I hoped you would," he said, and then I lowered the bucket into the swamp and he floated away. I saw his body drift a few meters, and then sink under the surface of the water.

When I returned home, I saw that a light was on in Leon's room. The door was open just a crack, so I knocked, and peeked in.

Leon opened the door. He was wearing Momma's favorite summer dress, and the flowered pattern flowed across him like a field. He wore her make-up badly, foundation clumping to his stubble, and eye shadow too thick under his dark eyebrows. Eyeliner ran in rivulets down his face.

"I didn't want you to know..."

"Say good-bye, then let her go," I said, calmly and seriously, and he put his arms around me, shuddering, as he exhaled.

The Frustrations of
Family 19

Simon crept up into the attic, where his parents stored the old photos, the Christmas lights, and all of Baba's things. Baba had died three months earlier, but no one had managed to go through her stuff yet, except Simon.

He knew what he was looking for. He had stored them away, underneath some of Baba's old dresses and shoes. He pulled out the small wooden box, and opened it up. The cards were wrapped in a sun-bleached silk scarf. He unwrapped Baba's Tarot cards, and shuffled them delicately. They were worn and faded, thin and brittle, like saltines, bloated from a flood decades past. Most of them had a blue stain on them, as if Baba had accidentally spilt ink on them ages ago.

Simon sat down on the metal trunk which held all of Baba's old photos. She had loved photos, loved to keep things just the way they were, as if imprinting their images on celluloid was as good as freezing time. She had boxes of photos inside the trunk, so many that no one even flipped through them, just stored them up in the attic. Simon was the only one who had glanced at them. He selected a photo of Baba taken only two weeks before she died. She was very old, grey skin contrasting against the bright colours of her wallpaper. She was so wrinkled that it looked like dark lightning was streaking towards the end of her nose. Simon stuck the photo onto the attic wall with a small wad of chewing gum.

Simon's mother's name was Margie. She used to sing in a swing band, outdated, but still stylish. She didn't sing anymore, not at all. Occasionally she would hum, whistle, or tap her feet along to a song on the radio, but she wouldn't sing. Now she cooked cakes, sewed, and basically kept the household in line. She would have liked to get a job, something exciting, like being a stewardess, flying off to different countries constantly, with a beautiful, spotless uniform. But Curtis, her husband, wanted the kind of wife who had dinner ready for him, a wife who kept the house in running order and took care of the children, a wife who didn't have a job.

Janey didn't have any friends, any human friends anyway. She did have Mr. Topcoat Weatherby, a tabby. She named him Topcoat for the black patch across his back and down to his front paws. She would call out of the back porch, "Mr. Topcoat Weatherby," and soon he would trot up, rubbing against her legs and mewing. Janey was scared of most everything, except the cat.

Simon softly placed seven cards down in a circle on the trunk. He had a book. It was Baba's before she died, and it still smelled like her, vaguely like a dishrag. He could look into the book and it would tell him what the cards meant. The first card was the Fool. He quickly flipped through the book, the pages soft and smooth with age, until he found the picture of the Fool.

The book said that the Fool card is the medieval court jester, who isn't afraid to say what he means. It also said that the Fool is the first step on the journey.

Curtis was a big man, burly, and with hands that didn't look like they belonged to a barber. They were tough, red and callused. They looked like they belonged to a plumber, or a butcher, or someone who worked with heavy machinery.

Curtis was in his barber shop, right beside Lloyd's Hardware and Sporting Goods on one side, and the store everyone called "the Chinaman's Grocery," which had a Coke sign sticking out the front, almost blocking Curtis' barber pole from view to people walking down Bluebell Street.

In front of Curtis was Mr. Anselm, an older man, in his sixties, with thin white hair, frizzy on the top with sides getting bristly. The sides were a job for the clippers, which he would buzz up the sides simply and quickly and effortlessly, but to get the top right, Curtis would use the scissors.

"So my grandson comes to town, and you wouldn't believe what he's done to hisself," the customer said, his voice grown hoarse and whiny with age, "he's got this earring in his ear! I look at him and say, 'what are you doing with that thing in your ear? You want for people to think you're a drug pusher or a pimp?' and he says to me that everyone is doing it these days, like I'm some old man who don't know what the young people are doing these days."

"Turn to the left a little, thanks. Oh shit, sorry, I dropped my comb," Curtis said, before plucking another comb from the tall glass jar of blue disinfectant, the barbicide.

"So I says to him, I says, 'Hey, you think you're so hip? My daddy had an earring when he was a sailor fifty years ago, and it ain't been in style since.' I swear, that kid looks like a damn poof."

Curtis clicked on the clippers, and held the vibrating blades close to the man's head, right near his ear, and slowly maneuvered it past a large mole on his temple, and upwards.

"Simon," Margie called to the attic, "Simon, lunch is ready." Simon quickly gathered up the cards and formed them into a deck. Simon was going into grade seven, and eleven years old. He had a crew cut, accenting his high hairline, and freckles across his nose and cheeks.

"Oh great Tarot cards, show me my card," he recited. He softly pulled a card from the deck. It was the nineteenth card. The Sun.

He opened the dishrag-smelling book, and searched for the explanation of the Sun card. He flipped around, and found it, the picture on the card reprinted in black and white, with the words "The Sun" in big bold letters above it. The book read "The Sun is a spiral, a spinning swirl of light and knowledge. But be careful, the light of insight may not be positive, but clouded over, like the sun hidden by winter and overcast skies."

"Simon!" Margie called again, her voice high pitched, "Lunch is getting cold. Hurry up!" Simon wrapped the cards in the silk handkerchief, placed them in the wooden box, and hid it beneath the pile of dresses again.

He raced down the stairs two at a time, spinning around the corner into the bright, clean kitchen.

"I'm here," he said, out of breath.

"Your hot dogs are getting cold. Now wash up and come to the table. And come when I call, right away. I don't need to be yelling all the time. It isn't good for my voice." Simon walked to the bathroom and ran his hands quickly under cold water, then wiped them on the white towels.

Janey was already at the table, picking at her hot dogs, eating more bun than wiener. She pinched off a piece of meat with her thin fingers, and dropped it down to Topcoat's waiting mouth. He bit into the hot chunk and chewed it down.

"What are you kids going to do today?" Margie asked.

"Tea with Mr. Topcoat Weatherby," Janey said, and then shook her head around, her pigtails hitting against her face.

"I dunno," Simon said. "Maybe go and see what's going on at the serious house."

"I don't like you playing with that weird girl and all those dead animals, Simon."

"She's all right. She can't help the way she is."

"Well, don't stay too long, and don't invite her over for dinner. I don't need to go through all the hassle of getting her into the house."

"All right, mom."

Simon walked up to the serious house. His and Lydia's houses were both on the same block, but the street was busy with traffic, so it was best to walk past her house, down to the corner, and cross there.

It was an old house, built in the thirties, with broken shutters and squeaky doors. The Shultz family moved into it a few years after Simon was born, and hadn't done much to fix it up. Occasionally there would be a plumbing truck in front of the house, other times a carpentry truck, or bricklayers, but nothing ever seemed to change in the serious house.

Simon walked up to the front doors, and knocked with the large brass knocker. After a few moments, Mrs. Shultz opened the door.

"Oh, hi, Simon," she said, smiling wide and toothy, her teeth crooked and wide gaps just after both canines.

"Hi, Mrs. Shultz. Is Lydia home?"

"Yes, she's reading in her room. You can go up if you want." Simon slipped off his sneakers and thumped up the wooden stairs. He stopped for a moment, looking at the Snowy Owl on the birch branch, eyes looking directly at him, never moving.

"Lydia?" he called. The upstairs was confusing. It was all doors and corridors, leading off into rooms he had never been into before. It seemed like every time he visited Lydia, the layout of the house changed, Lydia's room moved from South to North, the staircase led to a different part of the house.

"Over here, in my room." Lydia's voice came from behind Simon, so he spun around to his left to see her in her room, lying on her bed.

"Hi, Lydia, did you change rooms?"

"No. This is still my room."

"What 'cha reading?"

"Gormenghast."

"Sounds scary. How are you feeling?"

"I'm having a good day. Summer's ending though. Coming into another season of death, and school."

"Yeah," Simon said. School was hard for Simon, but more so for Lydia. Lydia was born differently. Lydia was born with the Mobius syndrome. She had only two fingers and a thumb on each underdeveloped hand, and she said she had three toes on each foot, although Simon had never seen her without her shoes laced up tightly on her small, stunted feet. The Mobius syndrome also meant that she was born without a certain nerve in her face, the nerve that allows people to smile. In all her life, Lydia had never smiled. This made things difficult at school. No one wanted to sit in a desk next to her, play with her at recess, or wheel her around in gym class. She sometimes met up with Simon at school, or played with Munroe Hope, the girl with only one ear, or the fat kid, Alec Forgie, who still picked his nose in class and once threw up in the playground and it went all the way over the monkey bars.

"Do you feel like doing anything?"

"No. Just sitting."

"Me too."

"I'll see you in a couple of weeks, Mr. Zimmerman," Curtis said as he dipped his comb into the tall jar of blue Barbicide. Mr. Zimmerman had short back and sides.

There was only one more appointment. Mr. Greaves at four-thirty. Curtis took out the broom and swept up Mr. Zimmerman's grey hair. At one time he'd worked with another barber, Eugene Petryk, but Eugene ran off with a cosmetologist from St. Paul, leaving behind a wife and two kids. Business had been good before that, and they'd had a boy named Sharkey come around and sweep up the hair. Sharkey was a tall blond kid, smoking at fifteen, but still responsible enough to get to work on time. Then they got a television installed so the customers would be entertained while they got their hair cut. But Eugene was gone, and Curtis couldn't afford to keep Sharkey on. Sharkey landed a job with the city, cutting lawns in the parks, and Curtis had to sweep up the hair himself.

Curtis stood up on a stool, and turned the television on. After a moment the blackness cleared, and was replaced by the wide green field of a pool table. There were only four coloured balls on it, two striped and two solid. The eight ball sat right in front of the side picket. Two men in tuxedos circled the table.

Curtis sat back on the barber chair and watched. Outside in the summer heat people walked by in short pants and light shirts, their hair unkempt and woolly.

"It's still summer," he said to himself, "what kind of fool would want long hair in weather like this?"

Curtis reached back and grabbed a steel flask from underneath the counter, and, turning his back to the front window, took a long drink.

On TV, one of the players hit the six ball, which spun badly off of the fifteen, nicking the eight gently into the side pocket.

"Aw shit."

Topcoat mewed over his empty dish. He looked up at Margie with his wide yellow eyes, staring.

"Janey!" Margie called, "Get down here and feed your damn cat already!"

Janey ran down the stairs, Barbie still in hand, and Topcoat turned around and mewed.

"Yes, Mommy."

"I don't know why we keep that cat. I told you when we got it, you have to take care of it, or we're giving it to the pound."

"I'm feeding it, Mommy," Janey said, scooping kibble from a large bag into the plastic dish.

"Not too much now. We spend enough on that damn thing. When you remember to feed it, it eats better than we do. We don't have a lot of money to spend on it. If it gets sick, we can't take it to the vet."

"I know, Mommy."

"Don't get too attached either. What if we had to move? We wouldn't take it with us. You can't change a cat's house. I read that in a book."

"Wendy moved here from Toronto, and she brought her cat."

"Cats can't change places. If they do, they go insane. It's the truth. Wendy's cat is insane. We should have gotten a bird."

"I like my cat."

"We should have gotten a bird." Margie dug her hands deep into the ground beef, massaging bread crumbs into it.

Topcoat ate half of the bowl of cat food, and strolled away, pausing to look up at Margie with curious eyes. Janey picked him up under his front legs and kissed him on the head. Then, cradling Topcoat like a baby, she walked upstairs to her room.

Lydia read out loud for a while, quoting sections of Gormenghast to Simon, and explaining what they meant. Lydia was the smartest girl in grade six.

"So," she said, pausing between chapters, "did the teachers have the talk with the boys yet?"

"What do you mean?"

"About sex. Have they talked to you about it last year?"

Simon looked at the ground, his eyes shrinking into his head.

"No."

"They talked to the girls. Carol Renaud started bleeding in Language class, and two weeks later we got the talk."

"Why was she bleeding?"

"Men-stroo-ation." She accented the words by holding her two-fingered hands up, palms towards Simon.

"What's that?" Simon frowned. He didn't like being left out of a secret.

"Women bleed between their legs. Every month blood comes out of our 'ginnys.'"

"No way," Simon said, feeling queasy.

"Yes way."

"Has it happened to you?"

"No. I don't even know if it will . Everything else of me seems to be mixed up, I wouldn't doubt it if I never do. I hope I don't."

"It sounds pretty gross."

"They said it was all part of our bodies' changing. Every woman goes through it."

"I'm glad it doesn't happen to men."

"How kind of you."

Simon looked close at her serious face. "Are you joking?"

"Yes."

Mr. Greaves arrived at four-twenty-five exactly. His crew cut was brittle and grey, only slightly shaggy over the ears, and a bit frizzy on the top where most of his hair had already fallen out. It was a contrast to Curtis' crew cut, which was perfectly trimmed, holding onto the dark brown of his youth, and full on the top.

"Afternoon, Mr. Greaves," Curtis said, standing up from the barber chair. He felt flush for a moment from the whisky.

"Hello Curtis. Could you please give me a haircut?" His voice was thin and ghost-like, he whispered and strained to speak.

"You have an appointment, you know."

"Yes, of course," Mr. Greaves said, taking off his black suit jacket. He was a tall, wrinkled man, with a bulging forehead and a fat bottom lip. "I guess I forgot I made an appointment. The nurses told me to come here, so I guess I wrote it down somewhere."

"What will you have?"

"Same as always, Curtis, just trim it up a little," he whispered.

"Okay, Mr. Greaves."

"You know, when I was young these corner barber shops had more customers. No one went and got their hair 'styled.' They just got it cut. You know."

"I know." Curtis wrapped a white towel around the man's neck, and then put on the plastic bib to protect his suit from the falling hair.

"There wasn't all these 'mop-tops' and 'boogie-cuts' all over the place, or 'Mohawks' either, you seen them? There were just two haircuts. The 'Brush' and the 'Crew.' And that's all we needed too," his voice grew louder as he spoke, but also more cracked and strained. "I can understand the women, getting their kids to drive them to Hazel's Coiffiers on Pioneer Street to get those perms, but men? Men?"

"Lean your head forward for a moment, please." He clicked on the clippers and they hummed quietly over the sound of the television.

"By the way, be careful around my ears. I was wearing my hearing aid, and then I fell down at the home, and the thing, it broke open on the back and gave me this terrible cut behind there. Look if you can."

Curtis glanced at the cut behind his ear. It wasn't long, but it looked deep, as if the broken plastic had gouged him rather than just sliced him.

"Oh shit, it looks like it hurts."

"I was walking, you see, and someone had left this tray in the hallway. Well, I was just going off to the poker game with Ernest and Stanley. Hey, do you know Stanley Punchatz? He comes here sometimes."

"Yes, I remember him," Curtis said, his hand jittery as he ran a comb closely up the side of his head, near to the wound.

"Janey!" Margie called up the stairs. A moment later, Janey raced down with a tiny teacup in her hand. The kitchen was filled with warm smells of meatloaf, and moist air from boiling potatoes and parsnips.

"Yes, Mommy?"

"Go over and get Simon. And don't linger either. Dad's going to be home from work soon."

"Mr. Topcoat Weatherby and I are having tea. We're talking about going to a fancy ball and dancing."

"The cat can wait for you. Run along." Janey reached up and placed the small teacup on the kitchen table, and walked into the living room. She buckled up her shiny black shoes and left the house.

Janey was wearing a red dress, the second brightest one she owned. Her favorite was her yellow dress, but she liked red too. It went down past her knees, and had frills on the hem and sleeves. As she ran down the street, she watched the frills blow around in the wind.

"What do you think happens to these things when they die?" Lydia asked, grasping the stuffed weasel in her small hands. Her wrists could barely hold up the weight of it.

"I don't know. Maybe the same thing that happens to us."

"Which is?"

"My parents believe that when you die, you go to Heaven and live with God. They say that all good people do, which is why we don't have to go to church."

"My mom believes that when you die, you're dead and that's it. You just lie in the ground and rot. There isn't anything, just blackness and rotting."

"Heaven is supposed to be all cloudy, and you never get bored and everyone is beautiful and can play the harp."

"My dad says that God is always watching. He says that mom is too clinical. All of us, even the little animals he stuffs, go to Heaven."

"Even the animals?" Simon asked. He couldn't believe that Lydia's father believed it. "Even my Uncle Walter's farm dog? With scabs all over his back and not even house-trained?"

"That's what he says."

"Wow."

"I don't believe in God. I think that everyone just makes it up so that they have someplace to go when they die."

"You don't believe in God? What if He heard you saying that?"

"He wouldn't. He doesn't exist."

Mrs. Shultz knocked on the door, and then opened it.

"Simon, your sister is here." Janey was standing behind Mrs. Shultz. "It's all right, Janey, you can go into her room."

"Hi, Simon," Janey said, and shuffled into the room around Mrs. Shultz, "hi, Lydia," she mumbled.

"What's up?"

"Mommy says that you have to come home now."

"In a minute. Sit down for a moment with us."

Janey looked over at Lydia, and quietly edged over to the bed. She sat down on the very corner, as far away from Lydia as she could. Janey looked around at all the animals; the crow in the corner which looked like it was studying her, the glossy salmon frozen into a twist, and the fuzzy weasel, eyes shiny but vacant.

"This is the first time you've been in my room, isn't it?"

"You aren't in your chair. I've only seen you in it."

"I have to sleep sometimes."

"We were just talking about what happens when you die," Simon said.

"We should go. Mommy said not to linger."

"All right."

"I'll talk to you later," Lydia said. "Give me a call tomorrow and maybe we can go to the park or something."

"All right. See you," Simon said, walking out of Lydia's room.

"You should come over sometime too, Janey. Maybe you could put my hair into nice pigtails like yours," she called, but Janey was already out of her room, and didn't call back.

Simon walked over to the staircase, but it was replaced with a doorway into the bathroom.

"This place always confuses me."

"The stairs are right here," Janey said, stepping down them one at a time.

Curtis took one last swig from his flask before closing up shop. He swept up Mr. Greaves hair, only bristles less than a centimeter long, and wiped the red vinyl of the chair. He stood up on the stool, wavering, and turned off the television.

He put on his thin coat and walked outside. It was only five o'clock. The store closed early most weekdays because the retirement home served dinner at five, and the sun was high in the sky. Not as high as the day before, Curtis noticed, but still high. Summer was still here, and that meant people wanted short haircuts.

Curtis fumbled for the keys, pulling them out of his jacket pocket and locking the door. Then he stepped out to his car, a blue Buick. He opened the side door and slid in. The car started easily, and Curtis revved the engine loudly a couple of times before cautiously pulling away from the curb.

"Now you kids be quiet when your father gets home. The last thing he needs is you two running around yelling," Margie said, spooning the over-boiled potatoes into a glass bowl.

"Mommy? Where's Mr. Topcoat Weatherby?"

"I don't know. He was around here earlier, but I haven't seen him."

"I'm going to look for him."

"No. Stay at the table," Margie said, but Janey slid off of her chair and raced up the stairs.

She checked through her room, under her bed and behind the dresser where he liked to hide sometimes, but he wasn't there. She looked into her parents' room, and then stuck her head into Simon's room.

Simon hadn't changed his room since Margie painted it when he was four. All of his preschool books were still in the shelves, filed between the Tolkien series and a book called *Medical Curiosities* he had found in Baba's stuff. The walls were blue with a rainbow painted across one wall, and a big pink cloud with a dark blue lightning bolt coming out from it on the other. Mr. Topcoat Weatherby wasn't in here either.

She raced downstairs, into the living room.

"Janey, come here right now," Margie said, more insistent. Janey looked behind the television where it was warm, and under the sofa.

Mr. Topcoat Weatherby was under the sofa, curled up in a ball. He looked up at Janey with his wide yellow eyes, and then prowled forwards.

"Kitty!" Janey yelled. She hauled the cat out and gave it a big hug. The cat pushed away from her, and Janey let him go. The cat leapt up onto the Lay-Z-Boy chair, and stood, obviously favoring his right front paw.

"Mr. Topcoat Weatherby, are you hurt?" Janey said, softly grabbing for the paw. The cat hissed, then moved forward and allowed Janey to pet him.

"Mommy, something's happened to the cat."

"Yeah, I saw it gimping around here earlier. I think it got its paw caught in something."

"He's hurting."

"I told you, we're not taking it to the vet. We can't afford it."

"I know, but he's hurting."

"The cat will lick it better. Cats don't have nerves like humans do. It doesn't feel anything. Come on, Daddy will be here any second, and we want to be waiting for him." Margie led Janey back to the table. Simon had his knife stuck between the prongs of his fork, and was pretending they were scissors. When they came into the room he put them down quickly, embarrassed he got caught.

"Is Topcoat all right?"

"He's got a hurt paw."

"That cat'll be all right. I swear, you two have nothing better to do than worry about that stupid animal." The soft purr of the engine reverberated against the house, as Curtis pulled into the driveway. "There. Your father is home. I'll get the meatloaf from the oven. Simon, you grab the potatoes, and be careful, they're hot." Simon took the potholders and carried the potatoes to the table. Margie followed behind him, and put the meatloaf on a placemat in the middle of the table. Then she got the parsnips, and put them in a bowl with a slab of butter on them.

Curtis flipped through the keys on his key chain, trying to find the right one. He passed by the shop key, the key to the shed, the key that he didn't know what it was to, and finally the house key. He stuck it into the lock and turned. It wasn't locked.

"Hello everyone," he called, walking in. He didn't take off his shoes, just walked right for the kitchen. "Hey, everyone's ready to eat, just like I like it."

"Hi, Daddy!"

"Hi, Dad."

"Hello, you two. Smells good, Margie."

"Meatloaf."

"Mmm." Curtis slipped off his shoes and sat down at the head of the table. "Oh. That feels good. I've been on my feet all day."

"Well dinner is right here," Margie said, smiling wide with her bright, perfect teeth.

"You forgot the ketchup," he said, peering across the table.

"Simon, get the ketchup, will you?"

"Sure mom." Simon hopped up and slid behind his father to get into the kitchen. He reappeared a moment later with the glass bottle in his hand. Curtis had already dished himself up the meatloaf, and was reaching into the potato bowl with his fork.

"Thanks, boy." Curtis grabbed for the other bowl. "Hey, what's with the carrots?"

"They're parsnips."

"Parsnips? Since when did we start eating parsnips?"

"We had them last Christmas..."

"Christmas is Christmas," Curtis said, his voice growing whiny, "I don't want parsnips. I want carrots."

"Well I just thought we would have parsnips again. We always like them at Christmas, and they're just like carrots..."

"Then why don't we just have carrots. I love carrots."

"Well if you don't like them, you don't have to eat them."

"Aw shit, I don't want to get into a damn argument the moment I get home. I'll eat them. I just like carrots better."

"Well sorry. I made parsnips."

"Parsnips. Pass me the ketchup.

After dinner Simon was back in the attic, the soft Tarot cards shuffled and ready. He placed them out one by one, noting that the first was the Five of Cups. He set the next six cards in a circle, the ten of wands, the eight of cups, two of cups, prince of swords, king of pentacles, and the Universe.

He pulled out the book, and looked up the Five of Cups. He read about unfulfilled hopes, disappointment, and confusion. Then he read through the rest, spending time studying each explanation in full. The descriptions were always a little confusing, like 'Liberation transformed into cruelty' and 'An initiate into esoteric mysteries.' Afterwards, he shuffled through the deck a few times.

"Oh great Tarot cards, show me my card," he recited. He softly pulled a card from the deck. It was the nineteenth card. The Sun.

Janey curled up in her bed and put her head under the covers. It was past her bedtime, but Margie and Curtis hadn't put her to bed yet.

"Oh, Mr. Topcoat Weatherby, I hope you're all right," she said, and kissed him on the head. Downstairs she could hear her parents arguing. It was the same nearly every night. Something would happen during dinner, something small. Sometimes it was her or Simon not being at the table when Curtis got home, so he could complain that Margie wouldn't even do him that favour. Other times, it was the wrong cut of beef, overcooked potatoes, or too much sage in the stuffing. Tonight it had been parsnips.

Janey held Topcoat as close to her as he would let her, only mewing softly if she accidentally rubbed his paw.

"All right, Topcoat, you watch and make sure I do this right. First I take off my clothes." She pulled her sweater and T-shirt over her head together, and threw them on the floor. Then she struggled with her button, but it finally came undone, and pulled her pants to the floor. She tried to step out of them, but her feet got stuck. "This is harder than it looks," she told the cat. She managed to tug her feet out of the pant-legs, and pull her socks off at the same time.

"Now I put on my 'jammies." She pulled open her drawer, and took out her soft sleepers, one-piece with feet. She climbed into them, and zipped up the front.

"See, not so bad." She climbed back into bed with Topcoat.

Simon came down from the attic, and heard his parents getting louder and louder in the living room below. He knocked on Janey's door, and opened it a crack.

"Janey? Are you asleep?"

"No. Mr. Topcoat Weatherby and I are talking."

"Good. You don't mind if I join you." Simon walked in, and sat down on the bed. "Did you change yourself?"

"Yes, all by myself. But Mr. Topcoat Weatherby made sure I did it right."

"That's good. Next time you should put your clothes into the basket. Mom seems to have enough problems just taking care of Dad."

"They sure are yelling."

"Yeah, Dad's breath smelled during dinner. I think he was drinking again. Anyway, you should be asleep." Simon got up, and walked to the door. "Do you want me to keep the door open and the light on in the hall?"

"Keep the light on, and the door closed."

Curtis was already gone before Simon woke up. School was still over a week away, so he was taking advantage of the extra time to sleep. He looked at his alarm clock. It was nine-thirty.

He put on his jeans and a blue and white striped shirt, and walked downstairs. The pant-legs of his jeans rode high above his ankle. The other kids at school had called him 'Floods.' He had asked his mom to let down the pant-legs, but she said that she wasn't going to do anything until his growth spurt was over. Simon hadn't noticed himself growing all summer, but she never lowered the hems.

"Finally up, Mr. Sleepyhead," his mother said, smiling her perfect smile.

"Morning, Mom."

"I kept breakfast for you. Here it is." She put a warm plate with two eggs, soggy toast and four pieces of bacon in front of him. "I let the eggs cook a little too long, so the yolk isn't runny like you like it."

"It's good," Simon said, laying a slice of bacon on the toast and taking a bite.

"Janey's in the back playing. I'm going off to Halperin's Foods for a while, so you'll have to keep an eye on her."

"I was going to take Lydia to the park."

"I don't like you spending so much time with her. You never know what can happen playing with someone like that."

"She isn't contagious. Anyway, I'll take Janey with us. You don't have to worry about her." He dug his fork into the yolk, and tore off a large hunk.

"Use a knife, Simon."

"Mrs. Shultz says 'hi.' She said to Mr. Shultz that you're looking good, and that you must eat like a bird."

"That's nice of them. Tell them that I say 'hi' back. Don't be too nice, though. I don't want them inviting us over or anything. Mr. Shultz is so odd, having to touch those dead animals all the time."

"I'll tell them."

"C'mon Janey, let's go pick up Lydia and head for the park."

"Yay!"

"Where's Topcoat?"

"We were playing, and he decided he wanted to go over into Mrs. Regula's garden and sniff around for a while. He said he'd be back later."

"He did, did he? All right. We'll see him when we get back."

Janey was wearing her favorite summer dress. It was the bright yellow dress, and all the way down to her knees. It had an orange collar and an orange hem at the bottom. The belt was the same yellow cloth, and came to a big bow on her belly. Simon took her by the hand, and they walked down the street.

Curtis was on his third customer of the day, and he had already started drinking. Mr. Creus was getting his crew cut touched up. He had grey skin, and his lips were deep burgundy, and they looked like a balloon left over too many days from a party, so the wrinkles are tiny and tight.

"There's this guy at the home who says that on the television they send these atomic rays that go into your head and it controls your mind," he said, spitting as he talked.

"You've been talking to Mr. Zimmerman, haven't you."

"That's his name, Zimmerman. He's off his rocker, he is. Heed my words, you can't trust them, not at all. There's this other guy, he thinks that the staff at the home, you know, they're putting stuff into the food so that we're all weak all the time, so that we don't go outside and run off or something like that."

"Turn to the left, please."

Mr. Creus craned his thick neck to the left. Curtis ran the buzzing clippers up the side of his head, the comb skimming softly across his scalp. Curtis' foot slipped, and he stumbled backwards.

"Aw shit!" he yelled.

"Hey! Watch it. You okay? Curtis?"

"Yeah, I just... slipped. I'm all right. Don't worry about it, it's these new shoes of mine, they have a slippery sole on them."

"I know what you mean. I got a pair of Oxfords down at the Army 'n Navy, and the heel comes right off of one only two weeks after I bought them."

"I'll take these ones back tomorrow."

Simon wheeled Lydia down the street to the park. Her wheelchair was old, bought second-hand, and rickety. The seat was hospital green, and there was a number, six, stenciled onto the back. Janey walked behind Simon.

"How the book going?"

"Gormenghast? I didn't read any more last night. After dinner I sat in the dining room talking with my mom. The doctor put her on medicine for her heart. My grandmother died of a heart attack. I guess these things can be passed on. That's one thing I don't have to worry about."

"You don't?"

"No. The doctor's looked at my heart through a big machine and they said it's all right. They check me over all the time. They said my mom has a heart murmur. That means that she could have a heart attack any time."

"What makes your heart murmur?"

"All sorts of stuff. Stress, thin veins, too much fat, all sorts."

"Wow. She could die."

"Yeah, but she won't. I know. She'll probably keep living until she's a hundred." She looked around her, "hey, is your sister still around?"

"Uh," Simon mumbled, as he quickly turned around. Janey was following close behind. "Yeah, she's still here."

"She's quiet."

"She's shy."

"Hey, Janey, why don't you walk up front here, so we can talk?"

"I was just looking at the cars."

"She'll be all right, Lydia, she'll relax and get more talkative when we get to the park. One time this guy came to the door selling stuff, and Janey opened the door. She took a look at him and hid behind the door, but he didn't see her, so it looked like the door opened all by itself. He walked in, and was calling around for anyone, so Janey raced outside and hooked the rake into the latch, so he couldn't get out."

"Poor Janey," Lydia said, her face perfectly emotionless, "she must have been scared."

"Yeah, well, the salesman sure was scared. He musta thought the house was haunted or something." Simon chuckled.

The park was just down the block from Lydia's house, but her parents rarely took her there. The park had two separate slides, a swing set with six swings, and a merry-go-round.

"Yay!" Janey yelled, running forward. She ran right up to the slide and started climbing. There weren't any other children in the park, just two teenagers smoking cigarettes on the pic-nic tables behind the wooden shed. Only the tough kids hung around the shed, carving their initials into the thick wood of the tables. Years earlier, someone had spray-painted 'Fuck' in big yellow letter across the green shed. The people of the neighborhood didn't want to spend money repainting it, so they spray-painted over it, changing the 'F' into a 'B,' and the 'u' and 'c' into 'o's, making it 'Book.'

Janey slid down the slide, yelling, and raced over to the swing.

"It's nice to see her run around like that."

"Well, maybe you'll run one day. You don't know what will happen." Simon looked close at her emotionless face. Sometimes when he looked at her, he swore he could sense some emotion, deep in her eyes. He looked, thought of longing and hope, but found nothing.

"Simon. Don't be foolish. I know that my feet will never change. They can't work; they're too small to support my weight."

"Well, you never know."

"I know. I won't change."

"Simon," Janey called, "give me a push."

"I'll be back in a minute." Simon walked over to Janey, who was kicking her feet back and forth, but getting nowhere. "I'm here, Janey."

"Push me. Please?"

"Yes," he said, pulling back on the wooden seat and then pushing her forward with all of his might.

"Whee!"

"Hold on tight now," Simon said, pushing her again. She kicked her feet out and swung higher and higher. Simon kept pushing her for a few minutes.

"Do an underdog!"

"All right, here I go!" Simon yelled, running underneath her as he pushed. He looked up, and the two tough teenagers from the 'Book' shed were standing in front of Lydia. Simon clenched his fists and stood there, until Janey nearly kicked him in the back on the following swing.

"Simon, watch out!" she called. Simon's face was turning redder. He started tromping towards the two teenagers.

"Janey, you stay here," he said curtly, as he sped away, up to Lydia and the two boys. Janey kept swinging back and forth, pigtails flowing in the wind.

"...wow," the taller boy with the raggedy jean jacket was saying, a lit cigarette hanging off of his bottom lip, "you really have it rough."

"Uh," his chubby friend said in agreement.

"Hey!" he said loudly, with only a touch of fear trembling, almost spoiling his bravado. "What's going on here?"

"It's all right, Simon. I was just having a lovely chat with these two young men here," she said, motioning towards them with a two-fingered hand.

"You have a really cool aunt, kid," the boy said, taking a long drag off of his cigarette, "See you later, Lyd."

"Yeah, see ya," his friend reiterated.

"I'm sure we'll meet again." Lydia kept her eyes on them as they walked out of the park.

"What did you tell them?"

"I told them I was thirty-seven, and that my disability made me look smaller and younger than I was. They believed it readily. I thought they looked kind of gullible."

"You said I was your nephew?"

"Well I had to come up with a reason I would be at the park with you, didn't I?"

"Yeah, I guess so."

Margie pulled out her shopping list. It wasn't any different than any other week, so she really didn't need it. She first went to the meat section, and checked through all the plastic wrapped meats, sitting lifeless in styrofoam plates. She picked out some pork chops, steak, hamburger, and minute steaks. Then she picked out a fat package of bacon.

She roamed up and down the aisles. She never missed out an aisle, even if she knew that she didn't need anything from a particular one. Her theory was that if she had forgotten something, seeing it in front of her would jog her memory.

She strolled down the cleaning aisle, putting a box of Spic-n-Span and a bag of blue and pink sponges into her metal cart. Then she arrived at the hair care aisle.

She picked up a box of hair bleach. It was the same brand she'd used to bleach her hair with when she sang with the band, the blond-haired beauty in the centre of all the attention. She would sing from her heart, the lights above her making her face glow radiantly, her lips beaming cherry red like a stop light. Her dresses had sequins sewn all over them, to reflect the light as if she were covered with fireflies, and behind her, eight handsome, well-kept men in tuxedos all working in perfect unison to keep the song swinging along. Best of all, each one of them was in love with Margie, each one watched her as she danced, spun, and sung for the audience. Oswald, the clarinet player, would have made a wonderful husband. His shoulders were wide and strong, his lips sensitive, eyes bluer than the sky. Or Mitch, the drummer, always active, his hands so fast.

She put the box back on the shelf, and walked forward. She never bought shampoo or other hair products, because Curtis could get them wholesale.

Janey took one last spin on the merry-go-round, and then walked back to Simon and Lydia. Simon was sitting cross-legged on the grass, picking fluffy-headed dandelions and blowing their seeds to the wind. Two families had shown up, so there were five other children in the park. A couple of boys were busy on the curly slide, and three girls were swinging. Janey decided it was time to go.

"I'm tired. Let's go home."

"Mom isn't going to be home yet, you know."

"I don't want to be here anymore."

"You could come over to my house," Lydia said.

"Yeah," Simon said, "let's do that." He picked himself up, and maneuvered Lydia back onto the sidewalk.

"There. The ride should be softer now."

"I don't mind a rough ride. It seems that everything is so flat anyway. Like the sidewalks and streets. I don't mind things bumpy.

"Keep up, Janey."

"I am."

"Maybe my mother can make us lunch. Do you like macaroni and cheese?"

"Yes."

"Well that's what we're having. Maybe my mother will let you have some. Would you like that?"

"Okay."

"Good," Lydia said, and then looked up at Simon. "What do you think?"

"Macaroni and cheese? Sounds good to me," he said, then pushed a little faster. "Ladies and gentlemen, please fasten your seatbelts. It looks as though we're coming into some turbulence here!" He started running, Janey running along behind him. "Are you enjoying this, Lydia?"

"It's fun," she said, face frozen in her permanent look of boredom. Simon took a sharp turn and raced up the sidewalk to the serious house.

Lydia's mother hadn't started making lunch yet. She was vacuuming the bearskin rug in the front room.

"Hi Mom. Can Simon and Janey stay for lunch?"

"Okay. It'll be about half-an-hour though, after I'm done with the vacuuming." She smiled wide, exposing the gaps behind her canines. Simon wondered how she got those gaps, thought of Mrs. Shultz as a child, eating too much caramel, or sucking her thumb too long. He wondered if there were something she could have done along the way to change it. "There's so much hair around here from this thing." She gave the bear's head a swift kick. "This one was shot out of season, so the hair keeps falling out."

"Don't kick it!" Janey shrieked, and then buried her face into Simon's back.

"Janey," Simon said, half-turning around, "don't worry, it doesn't feel anything. C'mon, let's go upstairs."

"Mom, could you help me upstairs?" Lydia asked. Her mother turned off the Electrolux with her foot, and then wheeled Lydia up to the stairs.

"You two can just go up to her room. We'll be up in a moment," Mrs. Shultz said. Simon walked up the stairs, past the Snowy Owl, and suddenly he couldn't remember which way Lydia's room was. He turned to the left, and opened a door. It was a closet full of shelves and towels.

"It's over here, Simon," Janey said, standing off to the right, in the doorway of Lydia's room.

"This place is so confusing."

Mrs. Shultz carried Lydia, over her shoulder, into the room, and slumped her down on the bed. Lydia pushed herself up with her small hands. "Thanks mom."

Simon came over and sat on the bed beside Lydia. Janey looked at the stuffed weasel.

"What do you want to do?" Lydia asked Janey.

"I don't know. Maybe we could pretend these were real," she said, holding the weasel up to the salmon.

"They are real."

"No they're not," Janey said, her mouth smirking in disbelief. She snorted, and then looked up at Simon.

"Lydia's right. They are real. They're dead, and Mr. Shultz stuffed them. He does that for a living. He's a taxidermist."

"These are real?"

"Yes."

"Then maybe we could pretend they're alive."

Margie drove the station wagon up the driveway. She stepped out of the car, and unloaded the groceries from the back. She carried two brown paper bags with her as she headed up the sidewalk, and struggled to unlock the front door. She dropped them in the kitchen, and went back for another two bags.

Then she saw Topcoat on the curb, the clotted fur and torn claws, mouth open in a silent cry. Topcoat had been hit by a car. His head was bloody, and his front legs jutted out behind him at bizarre angles, as if he were trying to hold his spine in place.

"At least someone had the decency to throw it to the side, so the crows don't get killed trying to pick at it."

She looked down at the body for a few moments. Janey wasn't going to be happy. She could hide it, and pretend that the cat had run away, but that might be worse. Or maybe she could just ignore it, and let Janey find him on the street.

Margie walked to the shed, and pulled out the rake. Gently, and with the sound of metal scratching on pavement, she slid the prongs under the cat. She lifted him up, and took him to the back yard. She dropped him in the flower garden, beside the fence.

Then she looked down on him. He looked unhappy, twisted sideways and misshapen. She flipped his back end over with the rake. Then she moved his head, so the bloody side was in the flowers. It looked as though the cat were sleeping instead of dead.

"Maybe this way is best."

"Janey," Mrs. Shultz called up to Lydia's room, where Simon and Janey were at a card table, Lydia had a breakfast tray she ate off of while still in her bed. The three children were finishing off the last noodles from their lunch. "Your mother is on the phone. She says she wants you to come home."

Janey shoved the last cheesy bit into her mouth. "Okay," she called back, mouth full of partially chewed macaroni.

"Thank her for lunch," Simon prompted.

"Thank you," she called again, this time dropping a few noodles from her mouth onto her plate. She quickly picked them up with her fingers and stuffed them back into her mouth. She got up from the table.

"Do you want me to walk you home?"

"No. I'm big. I can do it on my own."

"All right. I'll see you in a little while." Simon turned his back to Janey, and went and sat on Lydia's bed.

"Do you know what's in cheese?" Lydia asked. Janey heard this as she was just stepping out of the bedroom door, before she raced down the stairs and left the serious house.

Walking home, she noticed that there were a lot of birds out. They were all swooping over the traffic, spinning and diving through the air. Janey crossed at the corner, and started the walk back to her house. There was a large blue jay sitting on the fence of Mr. Holly's house, not flying away when she came near, just keeping a close eye on her, never blinking. There was also a flock of sparrows, clinging to Mr. Regula's crab-apple tree as if they were sucking the blood from it.

She finally made it up to her house, and a crow sat right on the peak of her house, perfectly silent, just sitting there. She walked in.

"Hi Mommy. I'm home."

"Hi Janey. Did you have a nice visit with Lydia?"

"We went to the park. I played on the slides, both of them, and the swing and the merry-go-round."

"That's nice. What did Lydia and Simon do?"

"Simon pushed me on the swing, and Lydia talked to some boys who were smoking cigarettes."

"Oh. Well, as long as Simon wasn't."

"He wasn't. He was just playing with me."

"That's nice then. So, why don't you go play in the back yard?"

"All right, Mommy."

Curtis took another deep drink of whiskey from his flask. It was almost empty. He had drunk far too much. It was only one o'clock and he was blurry-eyed, stumbling around the shop. It wasn't too bad though, as he didn't have any more appointments, and the shop didn't usually have anyone dropping in.

He placed the stool in front of the television, and stood up on it. As soon as the T.V. was on, he stumbled backwards and only just barely kept his feet about him as he crashed into the barber chair.

"Aw shit."

The television was set to a show where there was a man walking around in a dress. It looked as though it was supposed to be funny, but it was difficult to tell. There was the air of something serious about it.

"S'unnatural. S'what I think." He moved over to the stool again, but decided not to stand up on it. He kicked it to the side, and picked up the broom. He hit the television set with it, right on the channel changer. It didn't move, so he hit it again, and again. Then he hit it and accidentally turned it off. The door opened.

"Excuse me, are you open?" a young man asked. He was probably seventeen, with a ripped knee in his jeans and a stained yellow T-shirt.

"Yeah, course we're open," Curtis blurted, putting the broom down. The boy's hair was a mess. It was all matted and shaggy, bleached blond and brittle.

"Can I get a haircut?"

"S'a barber shop, isn't it?"

"Yeah," the boy said, smirking, "looks that way. Shall I sit down?"

"Go ahead. I'll be with you in a moment." Curtis pulled out a small brush and cleaned off his clippers, then turned around with them.

"So," he said, "brush cut?"

"Ha ha. No, not that intense. Can I get a mop-top?"

"Mop-top?"

"Yeah, you know. The top is long, and the back and sides are clipped short."

"I think I can handle it. You want me to cut off all the dead ends?"

"No. I like them."

"So," Curtis said, flicking the clippers on, "Don't think I've seen you 'round here before."

"No, I'm from out of town. Chicago, actually. My grandfather lives in the old folk's home here. He was born just outside of town."

Curtis looked down at the boy's ear. It was pierced.

"Your grandfather Mr. Anselm?"

"Yeah, how could you tell?"

"Family resemblance."

"Yeah. That's cool. I really like the old guy, except he just can't deal with the modern days. I mean, I only make it up here once every few years, and all he does is complain."

"You come with your parents?" Curtis buzzed the clippers up and around the back of his head. Every time he reached the point where the hair grew matted and long, he had to fight the urge to run the clippers all the way over his head, cutting everything short all the way to his bangs.

"No. They're living in Toronto. I don't see them at all anymore."

"So you came all this way to visit your Grandfather? That's nice." Curtis clicked off the clippers. There were a few mats in the back he was going to have to use the scissors on. The boys earring sparked brightly under the barber shop's bright lights.

"No, my band is up here doing a few gigs. I thought I would take a couple of days to visit. Gramps doesn't have that many years left. At least my parent's hope so. He's bleeding them dry with those retirement home payments. He always wants more money from them, says he has to drink in the bar because they don't allow alcohol in the home."

"I hear that. So what kind of music do you play?"

"Rock and roll. Loud and fast. But it isn't just brain-dead like all other forms of music, it's political. We want change, political revolution. We want to get all the old infirm white guys out of power and put in people who at least think, instead of just doing things because their archaic minds can't imagine anything new." Curtis' face grew flush, bright red, and his ears were burning hot. "I mean, look at all the dinosaurs running this country, driving it down with their corruption and closed-mindedness. I mean, look at the oppression. Out with the old, in with the new. We need change."

Curtis gripped the scissors tighter and tighter. The back was done. "Hold still." The scissors sliced through one of the pale, matted locks on the top of his head.

"What are you doing?"

Curtis didn't stop. He quickly sliced off another one, and it fell on to the boy's lap.

"Not the top! What are you doing?" The boy rocked forward, but Curtis held him back with his thick arm.

"Jus' clipping the dead ends!" Curtis sneered. The boy wrestled forward, nearly escaping his grasp, another lock falling to the floor. Curtis clung to the boy, and clipped once more, hard and fast, but no time to aim.

The scissors bit deep into flesh, and the top half of the boy's left ear fell to the ground. The boy screamed, horribly, clawing at his head. Curtis looked at it as if it were happening underwater. The ear fell so slowly, drops of blood spitting into perfect spheres as they splashed down, mixing with the hair clippings on the floor. Suddenly, everything was fast again.

"You fucker! You cut my ear off!" He grabbed at his head, only small smears of blood on his hands

"Uh, I didn't..."

"You... you fucker! I'm calling the cops!" the boy yelled running out of the shop.

Curtis dropped the scissors down to the ground, and just looked. The drops of blood mixed with hair were on the floor, and the scissors looked so bright, reflecting the bright light. Curtis pulled out his steel flask, and downed the rest of the whiskey.

Janey screamed. She wouldn't stop. It was high pitched and piercing, loud enough for the entire block to hear. Margie stood in the kitchen, slicing potatoes and listening to soft swing music.

Simon raced out of the serious house, and across the busy street, dodging cars as he ran. He raced past the rows of houses, turning in at his own, and leaping the gate into the back yard. Janey was still screaming.

She had Topcoat in her arms, cradling it like a baby. Her face was deep red, tears pouring from her eyes. She was drooling, her pigtails trembling in exaggeration of her head's shaking. There was blood all down the front of her yellow dress, and she was still screaming.

Simon stood there, just watching her. The neighbors were starting to walk onto their porches and peer over the fence at Janey.

"Janey," Simon said only loud enough to be heard over the scream, "Janey, stop. Breathe."

"Mr..." she gurgled, then screamed harshly again. She fell to the grass, crumpled into a ball around the dead cat. Simon knelt beside her, and put his arm around her. Janey's body convulsed with deep sobs, choking as she tried to breathe. "Topcoat..."

"I know," Simon said, putting his arms around her, holding her close to him, "you don't have to say anything."

"Weh...Weatherby."

"Maybe we should go inside. Can I take you up to your room?"

"I duh...don't wanna leave him."

"All right, let's just stay here for a while."

Inside, unable to stand the sound of her own daughter screaming and crying, Margie turned up the music, and whistled along with it.

The ambulance came first. The boy had run over to the retirement home, where the nurses quickly called the hospital, then proceeded to bandage up the boy's wound. Curtis could see the ambulance pull up to the home.

Curtis sat in his barber chair, the hair sticking to the bottoms of his shoes. His flask was empty, so he dunked it into the Barbicide, and was sipping the bitter liquid slowly. His lips were turning blue from the dye.

The police came next. They came up to the door, and knocked on the glass. Curtis had turned the sign from 'open' to 'closed,' but didn't lock the door. He motioned them to come in.

"Are you the owner of this shop?" the first police officer asked. He was an Asian man, thin with wide shoulders, and a thick mustache. He looked down at the blood and hair mixed on the floor.

"I am."

"And did you just cut the ear off of a customer here?" he asked, then, studying the floor, spotted the top half of the boy's ear. He walked over and picked it up with just the tips of his fingers, grimacing.

"I did."

"He's pressing charges against you," the other police officer said, a tall woman with short red hair, "for assault causing bodily harm. Would you please stand up."

Curtis staggered to his feet, his head was slumped forward, and his eyes shut. "All right, take me away."

The man walked behind Curtis and clipped handcuffs around his wrists. "Come with us," the woman said, "and we'll take your statement at the station. Do you want us to lock up the shop for you?"

"Uh, yeah. The keys are in my jacket pocket, over on the wall." The woman rustled through his jacket, and found his keys. Curtis was guided out of the shop, and she locked the door behind them. Curtis looked across the street at the retirement home, and all the windows were full of elderly faces, all staring out at him, each one with an individual look of disapproval.

"Did you see what this guy was drinking?" the Asian cop said.

"That blue stuff? Probably worse than Lysol. He smells like a brewery."

"We'd better get this ear to the hospital," he said, holding it softly between two fingers, as if the boy could still feel it if he pressed too hard. "Maybe they can sew it back on or something."

Janey was in her room. Simon had convinced her she would be better off inside. She was on the bed, shuddering, her body still convulsing with sobs.

Simon knocked on the door. "Janey?" he called, "I brought you some juice. Can I come in?"

Janey seemed to say something, but Simon couldn't make out what it was. He opened the door and entered.

"Here you are," he said, passing the tall glass to her. She took it, and, in between sobs, drank it all in one long drink. Then she wiped her mouth on her sleeve, and looked up at Simon. Her face was blotchy and red, her eyes bloodshot and glassy.

"Sit with me," she said, tears hanging in her eyes. Simon sat down with her. Janey held his hand, and Simon put his arm around her. She buried her head into his armpit. "What happens to you when you die?"

"I don't know. Mom and Dad say that you go to Heaven if you're good."

"Mr. Topcoat Weatherby was good," Janey said. She was crying again, inhaling breath in gulps.

"He was. Mr. Shultz says that animals go to Heaven too."

"What do you think happens?"

"I don't know. I guess I think you come back again, in some other body. I saw a show where people said they were Napoleon and stuff in other lives. It makes sense to me."

"Could Mr. Topcoat Weatherby come back again?" She looked up at Simon, tears running down her face again.

"Janey, there's no way to know. Maybe. What do you think he would come back as."

"Me."

"Yes, but you're you," Simon said.

"Then maybe he could be my baby."

There was another knock on the door.

"Janey," Margie called into the room, "I have a sandwich for you. Can I come in?"

"All right," Janey called. Margie walked in with a peanut butter sandwich on a white plate. "How are you feeling?"

"I'm sad. I miss Mr. Topcoat Weatherby."

Margie sat down on the bed, beside Simon, and handed the plate to Janey. She grabbed the sandwich off of it and stuffed a big bite into her mouth.

"The cat's gone, but we can get another one."

"I don't want another one," Janey said, she was starting to cry again.

"Well, maybe a dog, or a big colorful parrot. Would you like that? A great big parrot?"

Janey put the sandwich back on the plate and buried her head in her pillow.

"We don't have to talk about it right now, Janey," Margie said, "but you have to stop crying. It was just a cat. These things happen."

The phone rang downstairs.

"Simon, would you get that for me?"

"Yes mom." Simon walked out of the room.

"You see, it was just an animal. Your Grandmother died before you were born, and then we cried a lot, but she was a human. She had feelings and thoughts. The cat's probably happier dead. Animals don't have good lives."

Janey convulsed with deep gagging cries. She buried her head further into the pillow.

"Now Janey, I know you're upset. Maybe if you're really good, we can replace the cat with a new one."

"Mom," Simon called, racing up the stairs, "it's the police on the phone!"

Dinner that evening was quiet. After bailing out Curtis, Margie picked up ribs and fries from the greasy restaurant down the street. When they got home, Curtis stuffed a handful of fries into his mouth and headed upstairs. Simon nibbled at a rib while hearing his father vomiting into the toilet upstairs, then, thankfully, it sounded like he passed out.

Janey was crying. She picked at her fries, and dropped two ribs onto the ground.

"Janey," Margie said, "I think we've all been pretty lenient on you, but your crying is becoming annoying. Just stop it."

Janey stifled a few sobs, sucked in noisy breaths, but couldn't stop.

"All right, enough. I know you're sad, but enough is enough. Stop it."

"M...May I..." she sucked in another gagging breath, "be excused?"

"Yes. Go up to your room."

Janey ran from the table up the stairs. She glanced into the bathroom. Curtis was in his underwear on the bathroom linoleum, blue vomit covering his face and the floor. She looked at his back. He was still breathing.

She went into her room, and collapsed onto her bed.

"Mom," Simon said, "I think..."

"Simon," she cut him off, "let's just eat, all right?"

"Yes mom." Simon quickly dunked each fry into the blob of ketchup, and ate them. He left most of the ribs untouched. "I can't eat anymore."

"Then go up to your room and don't do anything. We've had enough trouble around here today." Margie picked up the dishes and took them into the kitchen. She placed them into the sink, and turned on the hot water. Then she flicked on the radio, to the swing station, and dripped the dishwashing liquid into the sink.

There was a song playing. It was fast, trumpet blaring along with trombone, the drums beating wild and fast. The words almost started bubbling up from Margie's mouth, great, high pitched songs. But Margie kept her mouth shut, washed the dishes in silence.

"I could go back," she said, imagining herself young again, the years seeming to slide away as she would stand on the stage again, the lights ignoring any wrinkles, tight dress of sequins and yellow feathers, the audience still intent on her every move. She imagined herself singing.

"I could go back anytime."

Simon walked up the stairs, and saw his father and the blue vomit. He was curled up and asleep. He looked so small in the bathroom, so naked against the sallow linoleum. He imagined Curtis was a small baby in there, a new life just choking for a first breath. Curtis coughed up a wad of blue phlegm, and it dripped from his mouth onto the floor.

Simon sat in his room for a while, looking through his old books, the ones he never had thrown away even when he grew too old for them. After a while, he went to see Janey.

The door was closed. He knocked. "Janey?"

"Yes?"

"Can I come in?"

"Are you alone?"

"Yeah."

"All right," she said, opening the door. She looked better, the glassiness gone from her eyes, although they were still bloodshot. There was a smudge of blood on her lip.

"What are you doing?"

"Promise not to tell?"

"What do you mean?"

"Mr. Topcoat Weatherby and I are playing."

"What?"

"He was so cold outside, on his back in the flowers, so I brought him in. He's under the covers with me. I'm warming him up."

Simon walked over and pulled up the covers. The dead cat was in the middle of her bed, front legs stretched upwards, as if grabbing for something no one could see.

"He was so cold out there. Look, his fur is still soft. We're going to have tea later, too. That should help warm him up."

"Janey, I don't think it's a good idea playing with Topcoat when he's dead."

"But look," she said, hopping into bed with Topcoat. She grabbed his front paws and waved one at Simon. She spoke in a high, squeaky voice, "hi Simon, I like playing with Janey. She's my best friend. Don't tell anyone, okay?"

Simon stood there for a moment, looking down at the cat. The blood on the cat's head had dried, and was clotting to the fur on his face, but the rest of him was soft looking.

"Okay?" Janey asked again in the high pitched cat-voice.

"Okay," Simon said, and then turned out of the room. He shut the door behind him, and then crept up the stairs to the attic.

He pulled Baba's shoes and dresses aside, and took out the small wooden box. He took the cards out, and unwrapped them from the pale red silk cloth. He shuffled them delicately, felt the brittle paper against the pads of his fingers.

He laid seven cards out in a circle on the blue trunk. The first card down was the Tower, the last, Death. He left them there, in the circle, not even looking up their meanings in the book.

"Oh great Tarot cards, show me my card," he recited. He softly pulled a card from the deck. It was the nineteenth card. The Sun.

"No," he said, then put all of the cards back into the deck, and shuffled rougher this time.

"Tarot cards show me my card." He pulled another card from the deck. It was The Sun.

"No!" he said, insistent. He put the card back into the deck and shuffled again. "Show me my card!" he said, and pulled another card from the deck. It was The Sun.

"Aw shit."

The Spirit Grove Cemetery

I'm looking through the shattered windshield of Mom's car. The half-empty bottle of rum has spilt onto the floor, and is making gurgling noises as it empties itself into the rubber floor mats. Grampa is in the back seat, unable to comprehend what is happening, and Mom... Mom is on the road, wearing that ratty robe, looking at the doe we've just crashed into. She's crying. She's drunk. I can't help thinking about my little brother, Oliver.

When Oliver was hit by Darren Collichuk's truck, I saw his tiny body fly through the air, arms pin-wheeling, legs as loose as boiled spaghetti, the sound of tires screeching to a halt. I had dived into the grass, because Darren's truck almost hit me as well, as it veered off the road and up onto the sidewalk. Oliver hit the pavement, and his skin scraped against the rough surface. Then, for the first time in my life, I saw a ghost.

It just jumped right out of Oliver's body. It was smoky-looking, and blurry. I squinted my eyes, and realized that it was Oliver. The body tumbled more, shoulders and back bloody, legs twisted into impossible angles, and Oliver saw it too. His form shivered, and he dove into the blood-streaked road. The body came to a stop, open eyed and lifeless.

Darren flung open the door of his truck. He was pale and shaking. He looked at me, but his eyes were lifeless too. He just stood there, staring at me, as if asking a question. I looked up at him from the damp grass, and couldn't answer. The moment seemed to last minutes.

Then every happened fast. His body jolted into action, and he sprinted across the street, to the parking lot of the Q-Mart, and leapt over the fence, running to Main Street and away.

Someone ran out of their house screaming. I don't remember who it was. Then another. They ran up to Oliver's body, but didn't touch it. Then someone came up to me. More people were around. I don't remember where they came from. I recognized some of the faces, like Bill Grudders who lived down the street, and Elma Bireme who worked at the Q-Mart. Everyone was moving so quickly. They grabbed me, and wouldn't let me look at Oliver.

"Cedric, please, don't look!" Elma Bireme said to me. It was too late, of course, I had been watching all along.

Then I screamed. It took so long for it to hit me, but I screamed high and loud, and it pierced the air louder than the truck's screeching tires. I started grabbing and fighting. Stanley McCready gripped me tightly, and he wasn't letting go. Tears were streaming down my face, blurring everything. I clawed and scratched, but they wouldn't let me go. I screamed louder and louder.

My screams were suddenly drowned out by a single piercing scream, louder than a departing train whistle. It was my mother. Someone tried to hold her back, but she tore through the arms, and knelt over Oliver's body. She touched his shoulder, gently, and then pulled away quickly, as if his body had burned her. Everyone was silent, even me. She slowly turned him over onto his back. His face was scraped up, and both his legs were obviously broken. She patted his hair and stuck it down with the blood. She leaned over and held him. The only sound was the ambulances wailing in the distance.

Margerie Canwell edged up to her, and put her arm on her shoulder. Mom whipped around, her nails bloody and red, and slapped Margerie across the face. I couldn't tell if Mom had cut Margerie with her nails, or if the blood was Oliver's, but either way there were four distinct bloody lines across Margerie's face.

"Keep away from me!" Mom yelled, her voice harsh and loud, and suddenly everyone jumped back into motion. People ran to get blankets to cover Oliver up, and others ran to get a doctor or anyone with medical training. We all knew he was dead, though. Everyone was talking about Darren Collichuk, how they couldn't believe he did this, and how he ran away. He must have been drinking, hopped up on pot, something. Other people were crying too. A couple of teenagers appeared on their ten-speeds, trying to see what was going on. Jimmy, who owned the tavern, yelled at them to go away. Mrs. Jacomb raced back to her house, where she left her own children playing unattended, and Bruce Gales said that he was going to tell the Collichuk's what had happened, and ran off to his truck.

Then, amid all the commotion, I saw Dad. He was just staring at Mom holding Oliver. He seemed so still, so much like a photograph. Tears streamed down his face, but otherwise he didn't move at all, and neither did Mom, hunching over Oliver's body, looking as though she were trying to keep it warm.

Stanley McCready looked down at me. I had stopped struggling, so he let me go, and held my hand. He walked me over to Dad. I felt like a robot, like cold metal.

Dad looked down at me, and then lunged at me. He held me so tightly that it hurt. He was shuddering, and slobbering as he sobbed.

"Thank God, Cedric," he mumbled into my shoulder, "thank God you're all right." I started crying again, and wrapped myself around Dad. He picked me up, and we stood there, shuddering, like a fragile tree in the wind.

It seemed like it took only seconds for the ambulances to arrive. The vans stopped, and suddenly five people in white uniforms leapt out and raced toward Mom and Oliver.

Mom picked Oliver up, and screamed at the medics.

"Go away, you're not getting him!" She held him with one arm, and clawed the air with the other. The medics looked at each other, wondering which one would take the initiative to get Mom to let go.

"Please, put the boy down. Moving him is the worst thing you can do," said a dark skinned woman in her white uniform. She was Aboriginal, and had short black hair and soft eyes. She approached Mom, but Mom was still fighting.

"Back, go away!" Mom's screams were cracking and she began sobbing. Dad put me down, and walked towards her.

"Put Oliver down," Dad said, "please, Judy, you have to let them look at him."

Mom looked at Dad like a small child deciding whether to share a toy. She moved, then hesitated, then gently laid Oliver down on the street. She stood up, and her dress was covered in blood and small bits of gravel. Dad walked up to her and held her, tightly, and they both clung to each other so tightly that their knuckles turned white.

Three police cars pulled up, and the Mounties rushed out. They ran up to the ambulance attendants, and asked four or five questions at once.

The ambulance people didn't answer. They swarmed Oliver's body, feeling for pulse, shining flashlights in his eyes. I stumbled, and found that I couldn't stand any longer. I sat down on the pavement. They pulled out a stretcher, and delicately maneuvered Oliver onto it. They talked in whispers, and put the thin blanket over Oliver's face. One of them said something to Dad, about a helicopter lift to Great Plains or something. Mom was shaking, and they let her come with them in the ambulance. They all jumped back into their ambulances and sped away.

The Mounties went to Dad, and tried to ask some questions, but he wouldn't answer. Then Stanley went up to one of them, and started mumbling out his version of what happened. He pointed towards Darren's truck, and the puddle of blood on the street. The Mountie went back to his truck, and spoke quickly into the radio.

The other Mounties were talking to people as well. Margerie Canwell, scratch marks across her face, was whispering to one officer, occasionally looking over at me with sad eyes. Elma Bireme was pointing over at the Q-Mart, where Darren ran by while making his escape. Elma kept shaking her head, as if she didn't believe the words she was saying.

One of the officers hopped into the police car and raced off, and another officer came up to us. She wasn't from Spirit Grove, but I had seen her around.

"Your wife has requested to go to the hospital with your son. I can take you too, if you wish."

"Yes, I think we had better go." Dad grabbed my hand, and we started to get into the back of the police car. Dad stopped, and called over to Bill Grudders.

"Bill. Go over to my house. I think we left the oven on." He sat down beside me, and looked blankly ahead as the car pulled away from the curb and drove down the street. I looked at my father, wondering how he could have remembered something so mundane as the oven. He didn't look at me, but he held me close to him.

The hospital in Great Plains was over an hour and a half away. The Mountie didn't try to make conversation with us, so the trip was very quiet. Except for the voices on the radio. The Mountie spoke once, after a volley of voices erupted from the radio, and then were quiet.

"Sounds like they caught the man from the truck."

"Darren," I said, but she didn't answer. Maybe she didn't want to jump to conclusions, or maybe she couldn't believe that Darren Collichuk had done something so awful. Everyone in town knew of Darren Collichuk. Everyone loved Darren.

We drove into Great Plains, and slowed down as the speed limit dropped from the highway. It felt like we were crawling along the main street, as if I could jump out and run faster. We passed by the Village Tree shopping centre, and the Kentucky Fried Chicken where we stopped for lunch most times we came to the town. The hospital was at the far end of town, through the residential sections built all at once, so the houses all looked exactly the same, rows upon rows of pastel coloured houses.

We pulled up, and got out of the police car. Dad pulled out his wallet, as if he thought he had to pay the Mountie for the drive, and then realized what he was doing, and put it away again. The Mountie got out of the car as well, and walked with us into the hospital.

As we walked inside, the antiseptic smell hit me directly, and I looked around at all the old people there. They were hanging around the lobby, sitting on the stiff sofas reading magazines. Some of them were patients, wearing white gown with ties in the back, but they weren't talking to each other. They all sat silently together, as if everything had already been said. We walked by them.

We were taken into a room, and Mom was already there. There was a sofa, and a television, and magazines. As soon as we came in, she stood up and ran to Dad. They held each other, and I started crying again.

"I'll find out what's going on," the Mountie said, and then she walked off.

Mom picked me up, and held me tightly. She was still wearing the bloody dress, but it looked like she had tried to clean it up a little. She was sobbing into my shoulders, and I wrapped my legs over her hips.

"Judy," Dad said, "what do you know?"

She looked over at him. "Nothing. I think he's..." and then trailed off into a long, sobbing bawl. Then the doctor came in. He had a sad expression on his face.

"I'm sorry. Oliver didn't make it. He passed away before he got here."

Mom gripped me so tightly that her fingernails dug into my back, but I didn't care. Mom whispered, "no... no... no..."

Dad stumbled, and fell onto the sofa. The doctor made a move as if the see if he was all right, and then stopped himself. Dad dug his fingers into his scalp, and clenched his teeth so tight I could see the muscles bulging out on his cheeks. His face was red with grief.

I was crying so hard my throat hurt and my eyes were sore, and Mom's grip on me hadn't loosened.

"If there's anyone we can call that would help..." the doctor trailed off. Dad sat up, and gulped breaths of air.

"Muh... my brother, Jack," he said, and then managed to tell the doctor Uncle Jack's phone number. "Tell him to check up on Grampa."

"Just talk to a nurse if you need anything. I'm available to answer any questions you may have. I'm deeply, deeply sorry." The doctor walked away, and shut the door behind him. We sat in that small room, all of us crying uncontrollable, for at least an hour. Then we asked the Mountie to drive us home, and she did.

Dad sat in the front this time, and Mom and I sat in the back. She held me the entire way.

Uncle Jack was at the house when we arrived. He came out onto the porch as soon as the car pulled up. Dad got out, and he and Uncle Jack hugged for a long time.

"How is Judy's father?" my father asked Uncle Jack.

"I told him what happened. I don't think he understands."

Mom and I walked into the house, and she went into Oliver's room, and shut the door.

There were flowers on the living room table. One of the neighbors must have picked them and given them to Uncle Jack for us. The fridge was full of casseroles, all covered with tin foil, wrapped up tight. I guess the first thing people do after a death is cook. I sat down in the living room and waited. I couldn't cry anymore. I just wanted to stop thinking, to be free of pain. Dad and Uncle Jack came into the house.

"Where's Mom?" Dad asked.

"Oliver's room," I said. Uncle Jack sat beside me on the sofa, and Dad went into Oliver's room, and he too closed the door behind him.

"Are you all right, Cedric?" Uncle Jack asked me. He smelled like cigarette smoke, and hadn't shaved. He was larger than my dad, and wore dirty jeans everywhere. He used to be cleaner, used to shave and comb his hair and wear fancy cowboy boots and neatly pressed plaid shirts before Auntie Emma died of cancer. He had soft eyes, and wasn't wearing a baseball hat like he normally did, so I could see his balding head, the greasy wisps of pressed against his head.

"I don't want to think."

"I know. I didn't want to think when Emma died. I just wanted to sit and... nothing. Just... nothing."

I didn't say anything, but nodded in agreement.

"It gets better. It does. I know it doesn't feel like it will, but you do get over it."

The tears welled up in my eyes again, and Uncle Jack stopped talking for a moment. He put his arm around me, and I could smell his strong odor. It didn't smell bad, but the cigarette smell clung to my nostrils.

"Say, are you hungry? There's a half-a-dozen casseroles in the fridge, and the freezer has plates of food in it from the neighbors."

"I don't know. Can we watch television?"

"Sure," he said, and got up and turned on the TV. He turned it to some talk show or something. I couldn't concentrate on it. I just tried to relax my brain, and not think of Oliver. I couldn't hear Mom and Dad.

Uncle Jack stood up and stretched his back. He looked around uncomfortably, rubbing his butt with his hands.

"I'd better go check up on your Grandfather. Do you want to come?"

"Yeah, just for a minute," I said. I normally hated checking up on Grampa, he was such a burden.

Grampa lived in our garage. Dad fixed it up for him, with heating, and a good floor, and made three rooms in it for him. I always remember it smelling. At first it smelled like gasoline, then like glue and fresh paint, and then like Grampa. Uncle Jack knocked on the door.

"Mr. Gardner?" Uncle Jack called. Then he turned the doorknob, and we walked in.

"Mr. Gardner?" he called again. Grampa was sitting on his sofa, just staring at the wall. He was wearing a burgundy sweater, and his thick bifocals were perched on the end of his nose. He was holding a copy of Reader's Digest, the same one he had been reading for two years.

I sat down beside him.

"Oh, hello there..." he said. He looked at me closely, smiling with his yellow teeth. I snuggled up to his arm. His sweater was soft. He didn't know me. "Daniel?"

"Cedric, Grampa."

"I'm just seeing if you are all right," Uncle Jack said. Grampa jolted, and then stood up. He turned to Uncle Jack and stuck out his hand.

"How do you do, I'm Eli Gardner."

Uncle Jack shook his hand, as I had seen him do a hundred times. Uncle Jack didn't meet Grampa until after Grampa started forgetting things.

"Jack. How do you do?"

"Very good, would you like some tea? Sarah is around here someplace..." he drifted off. Sarah was my grandmother's name. She was dead.

"That's all right, no tea for me," Uncle Jack said. Grampa sat down again, and picked up his book.

"Well," Grampa said, "I think I might go for a bicycle ride later. It looks like a nice day."

"No Grampa, no bike rides." Grampa loved to ride his bicycle around town, but he wasn't very strong anymore, and always got tired and fell over. He would forget where he lived, sometimes ending up at the empty lot where the house he grew up in used to stand. He would end up yelling that someone stole his house, and then George Dillman, the man who lived next to the lot, would bring him back. Then Mom and Dad would argue about sending him to the home again. It always happened the same way.

"Maybe tomorrow then?"

Uncle Jack took my hand, and we walked back to the house. As we passed by Oliver's room, I could hear Mom crying. I wanted to go in, but I didn't. Uncle Jack and I sat in the living room watching TV. I don't remember how much time passed, or how many shows we watched, but he brought out some rice casserole for us to eat, and I remember him taking me to bed. I had fallen asleep in front of the television.

The next morning I woke up, and started to get dressed. Suddenly I remembered Oliver's death, and I started crying again. I felt awful, and spent the entire morning in my room, all red-eyed and snotty. When I stopped crying, I came out.

It was Sunday, and we didn't go to church that morning. Mom was walking around, making lunch. She set the table, bringing out a plate for Oliver, and then taking it back to the kitchen. We had toasted tomato sandwiches. Uncle Jack wasn't over.

After we ate, I brought Grampa his lunch. He didn't like toast, so he just got a tomato sandwich with white bread, and a bowl of creamy soup. He was always happy when he got his meals, so I didn't mind bringing them so much. He was still reading the Reader's Digest.

When I came out, Colin was in the back yard. Colin was my best friend, along with Wayne. We were the best hockey players in grade four.

"How are you doing?" He asked. I smiled, but tears welled up in my eyes again, and my bottom lip started trembling. I sniffed back my runny nose, and rubbed my eyes.

"I'm all right."

"Here," he said, handing over a paper Q-Mart bag, "I brought you some of my toys to play with. You can borrow them for as long as you want." Colin's Dad always got him the best toys, because when his parents got divorced he moved to Vancouver, and sent him back all the cool stuff. He had a BMX bike and a skateboard, and a remote control dune buggy that went twenty miles an hour. I looked into the back, and there were three transformers and his Star Wars action figures. Really good stuff.

"Thanks Colin."

"Hey, Wayne and me are going to get some kids together and play street hockey tonight. Are you in?"

"Yeah. Maybe. Where?"

"The tarmac." He smiled at me. The school didn't like the kids hanging around when it wasn't a school day, but they couldn't do anything about it. They always thought we were going to break something.

Colin walked away, and I went into the house. Oliver's door was closed. Dad sat me down on the sofa.

"They have Darren in jail in Great Plains. They caught him running away through Mike Jenken's field. He's going to see a judge, and they'll probably let him out on bail tomorrow morning."

I couldn't believe it. They were going to let him go? He killed Oliver, and nearly killed me to? I tried to speak, but the words caught in my throat, and my face turned red. Dad saw that I something was going on, so he grabbed me and held me tight.

"Don't worry," he whispered, "he's in trouble. He'll be in jail for a long time."

I started crying again. I wanted him to go to jail, but it wasn't enough. I wanted him to get hit by a truck. I wanted him to be killed. It was only fair for him to be killed.

Oliver was buried on Tuesday. Monday felt all blurry, like I dreamt it. I didn't go to school, and Dad didn't go to work, so we all stayed indoors. I didn't play street hockey.

It felt weird to go to church without Oliver. Everything felt weird without Oliver, but church especially. Oliver didn't like church, because he always squirmed and wanted to go outside. He would start whining half-way through the sermon, and Mom would look around, all embarrassed, and whisper into his ear. She would whisper to him for minutes on end, maybe little stories, maybe songs. I never found out, and she didn't whisper to me that way when I was his age.

When we got to the church, the entire town was there. They were all lined up outside, and it was a chilly day too. They parted as we got out of the car, and everyone was silent. I started crying again. Mom and Dad looked sick. Mom was helping Grampa, because he didn't walk so well anymore.

We went to the front, and sat down on the wooden pews. I had never sat in the front before, but I don't remember exactly what it was like. It just felt like a different building, like a building that didn't really exist. Everyone else piled into the church, and not everyone could fit. They were standing in the back, and even in the doorway and on the front steps. The Collichuks were there, silent and ashamed. When I looked at them, I felt my heart stop for a moment. They looked worse than Mom and Dad.

The sermon started, and I suddenly realized that there was a coffin. I don't know how I missed it. The top was closed, but I knew that Oliver was inside of it. My hands went numb, and I couldn't think straight. It was like the priest was speaking in a different language. We stood up, and sat down again. We prayed, sang something, and cried. I never saw so many people crying. Even people we hardly knew were crying. Elma Bireme was crying, and she didn't even cry when it happened.

Then it was over. We stood up, and they took the coffin into a big black car, and we drove to the cemetery.

The Spirit Grove cemetery is just up the hill from the school, but we're never allowed to go into it. There is a white wooden fence around it, about waist high, so it isn't tall enough to obstruct the view, but let's people know they shouldn't be in there. It isn't very big.

They took Oliver's coffin out of the car, and we followed them as they walked it to the grave. It was chilly out, and the wind was blowing. The little cemetery was full of people from town, all silently listening. The priest talked some more, and they lowered Oliver into the hole.

But I couldn't concentrate. There was so much happening. It seemed like everyone was there, and the coffin looked so small. The trees were all rustling, and everyone was bundled up.

And there were wisps of white smoke, or mist, or something. I would catch glimpses of faces in the crowd, and then they were gone. I felt sick to my stomach, and my throat ached so badly I thought it would never feel good again, and Oliver was dead.

On Thursday after they finished school, Wayne and Colin came over. I don't remember them knocking on the door or anything, just coming up to my room, and saying hello.

"There's a couple of guys getting together for street hockey. Do you feel like playing?" Colin asked. Wayne just stood there, totally silent, looking at his feet. I was really glad they came over. I couldn't stay in the house any longer. Mom and Dad were just eating and sleeping, and I couldn't even concentrate long enough to watch TV. I was bored.

"Yeah, that sounds good," I said, although I was scared. I hadn't done anything outside since the funeral. The closest I got to leaving the yard was bringing Grampa his dinner.

I got off my bed, and took my stick out from the closet.

"Yeah!" Wayne said. He was grinning like an idiot. He must have thought that I was over Oliver's death or something, like it was a great breakthrough that I was bored and wanted to play street hockey. I still felt like crap.

Mom and Dad didn't react when I told them I was going out. Dad just said, "Fine. Dinner is at six." I wedged on my sneakers without untying them, and we left.

All the regular hockey players were there, like James and Simon Drakes, and Billy and Bobby, the Chonter twins, and Cindy Perks, the only girl that could play hockey halfway decent. We split up into teams, with me on one, and Colin on the other. We were the best players, so if we were on the same team we would be too good. We always played on opposite teams, and we were always the forwards.

We didn't have a puck. Normally, we used either a puck or a ball. Street hockey is best with a ball, because it rolls and is hard for the goalie to block. The puck always stops short on the tarmac, but it will do in a pinch. Wayne's dog chewed up his soft rubber puck, and no one brought a ball. Luckily, Wayne stole the dog's rubber hamburger dog toy. It was pretty stiff, and rolled unpredictably, so we played with that.

I was playing crappy. The hamburger was hard to hit, and I couldn't seem to follow what was going on. Colin scored three goals easily. We hardly got a shot on net.

Cindy Perks came onto our side, and she took over as the centre. I shifted over to defense, and Bobby Chonter took the wing. We had a better team then, and Bobby scored a goal. We didn't suck so badly with Cindy on the team.

The hamburger was on the other side of the tarmac when I looked up to the cemetery. Someone was up there, and it looked like they were standing next to Oliver's grave. I dropped the stick, and walked up.

When I got there, no one was around. I was watching the gate, and no one left, so I couldn't figure out what was going on.

Colin puffed up the hill.

"H...Hey Cedric, what's up?"

"Did you see someone up here?"

"No. I was playing. I scored a goal."

"I thought I saw someone. Someone standing around in the graveyard looking at the tombstones."

"Maybe it was Mr. Peedee." Mr. Peedee was the school janitor. He also took care of the cemetery, and did carpet cleaning.

"Yeah. Maybe."

Colin's team won, of course, even though they didn't count the goal he got when I went to the cemetery. He and Wayne walked me home. I was actually having a good time playing hockey, and then I remembered Oliver. He used to want to play with us, but he was too young. Every so often we would let him play goalie, because at least there was a chance that the ball would deflect off of him. At home we would tell Mom and Dad how good he was, sometimes putting Old Dutch chip boxes over his calves to pretend they were goalie pads and telling them he was going to be a goalie when he grew up.

The house stunk. I said good-bye to my friends and walked it, and it smelled really bad. I hadn't noticed that the dishes were stacking up, and that no one had cleaned since Oliver's death.

Mom was drinking in the kitchen. She had a bottle of wine in front of her, and a drinking glass full of the red liquid. Her hair was all messy, and she had a big red stain on her T-shirt. She smelled, too. I knew not to hang around too long.

I went upstairs, and sat down on my bed. I didn't know where Dad was. As it turns out, he had to run to the grainery on some kind of emergency. There was some valve or something that wasn't working. They couldn't figure out how to fix it.

It was way after six when Dad finally got home. I heard him pull up, and watched him, from my bedroom window, walk into the house. He and Mom were talking in the kitchen, and they sounded like they were arguing. It was hard to tell, because Mom was crying and I couldn't really make out what either of them was saying. I decided to stay in my room and read. I fell asleep without dinner. It didn't matter.

Monday morning I had to go back to school. One week off was all my parents would allow. Dad went back to work too, but Mom stayed home still. Colin and Wayne were in my class, and we sat in the back so we could whisper without getting caught all the time. Everyone kept looking at me. I was the kid with the dead brother.

Mrs. Cohen was our teacher. There were only enough students for one grade six class, so she taught us all. She was a thin, wispy woman with grey hair and a seemingly inexhaustible supply of ugly brown dresses. She was nice, but too strict.

We started off every day reading. For the kids who didn't have a book, she had a supply in a book rack at the front of the room. Wayne always took the book of Superman Trivia questions. He memorized them all, and there was nothing about Superman that he didn't know. Unfortunately, he didn't know too much about anything else, and he kept failing tests. Luckily, no one except the real dummies ever failed.

I liked reading. I was always into some book, like Bruno and Boots, or Doc Savage, or Conan. I liked the adventure books best. Although I was reading this really great book about Wayne Gretzky. It had pictures of him, and all his hockey stats, and how he grew up and stuff. I was halfway through, and it just kept getting better.

I kept reading right into Math, but then Mrs. Cohen caught me and made me pay attention. I didn't understand what was going on. They must have all learned new stuff during the week I was gone. It didn't make any sense.

After school Colin and Wayne decided to play a quick game of kick-ball, which is basically keep-away except you try to keep the ball away from everyone else. It never lasts long, because either we get frustrated, or Wayne gets the ball and kicks it onto the street. Wayne is the best kicker in grade six.

We said good-bye, and they started walking towards their homes. I decided to go see Oliver's grave. I missed him. I mean, he was a complete pain when he was alive, always crying and getting in the way, but when he was gone, I realized that I really loved him.

I walked into the cemetery, and went to his grave. The air was chilly, and it smelt like winter was approaching. The dirt on his grave was still fresh.

"Hi Oliver," I said. I became really self-conscious, and kept quiet. It felt like I was being watched.

I thought I heard someone crying, like a voice on the wind, but couldn't pinpoint it. There was this weird feeling in the air.

Everything was getting hazy, like a fog was rolling in. Then a form appeared in the mist.

I ran as fast as I could. I jumped over the wooden fence and ran down to the school. The cold air was making it hard to breathe, and I coughed loudly a few times.

When I turned around to the graveyard, there was no mist, no fog, nothing. I was really scared, so I ran all the way home.

Mom had cleaned up the dishes, and the house didn't smell so bad. She was still looking haggard, but she was up and about.

"Cedric," she said, "go and spend some time with your grandfather. He's all alone out there."

"Mom, do I have to?"

"You can bring a book along if you like."

So I went up to my room, and picked out a book of 1001 jokes. Then I went to see Grampa.

He was sitting in his house, reading his Reader's Digest. He was all wrapped up in a yellow blanket with green flowers on it. Grandma sewed it.

"Hi Grampa," I said, and sat down next to him. He looked at me and smiled, warmly.

"Aren't you Sammy Witzer?" he asked.

"No. Cedric. Your Grandson."

"Well, isn't that wonderful. Maybe we can get you some cookies or something. Sarah is around here someplace..."

"No Grampa. She isn't."

"Oh... Oh, that's too bad. That's really too bad."

"Grampa. I'm scared."

"Scared of what?" He was looking deep into my eyes, and he seemed so clear headed, so with it, like his memory may be gone, but he was still thinking clearly.

"Grampa. I'm scared of what happened to Oliver. I'm scared what happens when you die."

"My, that is a big concern, isn't it."

"I think I saw a ghost, Grampa. Maybe it's Oliver. Maybe Oliver is a ghost."

"Oh. I don't know Oliver. Was he a friend of yours?"

"He's my brother, remember? He's dead now." Tears formed on my eyes, even though I had decided that I wasn't going to cry anymore.

"Well, young man, let me tell you a story. When I was a boy, about your age, my grandfather lived just down the road from us. He had been a baker in town here, but then when he stopped baking he moved back to his old homestead. I would visit him and he would give me fresh baked buns, with butter that he churned himself. He had to make fresh buns all the time, because they were soft, and he had lost all of his teeth, so he couldn't chew. One day I visited him, and he wouldn't answer the door. He just looked at me through the window, and smiled. What was really weird was that when he smiled, he had a full set of teeth. I went home, and found out that he had died the night before, in town, and that he hadn't been anywhere near the house. So, you see, maybe he was there, maybe I imagined it. There's more that goes on that we know."

Then Grampa looked forward, like he was trying to remember something else, but couldn't. His lips were deep cherry red, and he mumbled out a couple of words, and then went back to his book.

I went back into the house a couple of hours later. Dad was home, but he was working in the den. Mom was in bed, so I watched TV until suppertime.

I didn't go back to the cemetery the next day. In fact, I didn't even look up there during recess, didn't play hockey on the tarmac, didn't even go behind the school at all. I stayed in the front with all the girls, watching them spin around on the monkey bars by their knees. Boys couldn't do that. Maybe it has something to do with the differences between boys and girls, but I've never seen a boy able to spin around by the knee like that.

They whirled around, their pony-tails like streamers out behind them. I just sat and did nothing. Wayne and Colin were probably out back, sticks in hand slap-shooting pine cones, or whatever else they could get their hands on.

The girls wouldn't come over to me. Normally they would, but I was now the kid with the dead brother, and everyone was afraid of me. They thought that if they would come up to me, I would start blubbering and end up in a mental asylum. They might have been right.

Math class was boring, as usual. I can't understand how multiplication is going to help me in the rest of my life. How many times are you going to have five groups, each with exactly seven items in them? If you went to the bother of counting each group to make sure they all only had seven in them, why not just count them all together? I have trouble understanding things that are pointless.

After school, Wayne said he was going to tape up his stick, and wondered if I wanted to come over and watch. Boring as it sounds, it seemed like a better idea than going home. Unfortunately, that meant walking by the cemetery. It was cloudy too, and since winter was coming, that meant it was already getting dark out.

"Come on, it'll be fun," Wayne cajoled, "Colin's coming. We could even play slap shot in the driveway. I'll be the goalie."

"Yeah, sounds fun." I mustered up the courage, and smiled confidently.

We walked around the corner of the school, and Colin was making jokes about something stupid, I can't even remember what, but my eyes betrayed me. I looked directly up into the cemetery, full on. There were four or five forms, wispy and unreal. They were spirits, and I couldn't take another step. I just stared up at them, moving without walking, almost transparent, pale, sunken eyes and bony shoulders. Colin turned to me.

"Cedric, man, what's the matter?" He stared at me. I must have gone totally pale, and was sweating in the chilly fall air.

"Cedric," Wayne said, "you ok?"

"I can't come over," I said. Tears were welling up in my eyes, I don't know why. "I got to go... I can't..." I mumbled, and stumbled backwards, around the school. Then I took off, really running. Colin and Wayne looked at me, and then up at the cemetery. I don't think they saw anything.

When I got home, Mom was drinking again. I don't know what she got into, but it smelled horrible.

"Hey! Cedric! You're late from school. What happened? Got in trouble for kissing girls? Hey?"

"No Mom," I said. She was wearing a robe, and her hair was a mess. She was holding the bottle in her hand. There was a huge stain down the front of her robe, and her socks were half-hanging off of her feet, one soaked and rope-like.

"Look, you better take care of yourself," she grabbed me by the shoulder and looked me right in the face. Her eyes were watery and bloodshot. "Listen! You're a good kid. Don't you get in no trouble now. You make Mommy proud. Eh? Eh?"

"Sure Mom. Can I go to my room now?"

"Yeah. No, wait. Go see Grampa. Make sure he took his medicine."

"All right Mom," I said, and turned around to go back outside. The air outside smelled much cleaner than inside my house.

Grampa was sitting in the garage, drinking tea. I knocked on the door, and came in.

"Hi Grampa."

"Well, hello there little guy. Have you come to visit me?"

"Yeah. I guess so. Did you take your medicine today?" I asked. He looked as though he was thinking for a moment, and then went back to his tea. I went into the kitchenette and opened Grampa's pill drawer. There were five or six bottles, and a small plastic container with the days of the week on each small section. Today's was empty.

"Grampa? Do you have a television in here?" I asked. I had never really dug through his stuff. It all came in boxes, and Mom and Dad set it up for Grampa.

"Television? I don't really like those new things. They're all noise and flashing lights."

"All right Grampa. Do you want to read?" I asked. I saw him looking for his Reader's Digest, so I quickly distracted him. "How about this one? Zane Grey? It's a cowboy book." It made me sad to see him reading the same book over and over again, every day. So pathetic.

"That sounds good. I think I read it before once, a long time ago..."

I pulled out a comic book from the pile I had stashed in Grampa's house earlier. There wasn't much else I could do hanging around with him. He got up, and turned on some music on his tape deck, old country music, but I didn't recognize who it was. I hated country music, but I didn't say anything. Then he sat down, and started reading.

After an hour or so, I decided to leave him to his book. I went into the house, and Dad was home. He and Mom were arguing, so I went up to my room. I could hear their voices, but couldn't make out what they were saying. They were angry though.

I was getting too hungry to stay upstairs, so I snuck down to the kitchen for a sandwich.

"...and why do we have to keep your father here? You can't even take care of yourself..." my father said, his voice sharp.

"Listen, just because yours are dead, doesn't mean I don't care for mine. He doesn't want to go to the home..."

"Christ Judy, at least he would get three meals a day, and wouldn't have to live in an old garage."

"He likes the garage. He likes living here. Don't you fucking dare try to get rid of him."

"It still smells like gasoline in there. You're not being rational."

"Always me. I'm not being rational. I'm the drunk. I'm not dealing with my problems. Well what about yourself! You're just a coward who shuffles into work every day and is too scared to ask for a raise! Maybe if you made more money, we could build my father a decent place to live..."

"This is pointless. You can't see how ridiculous you're being."

"I can't see. Again, pointing it at me."

"It is you. You're turning into a drunk. Look at yourself. You're some sloppy old souse like those bitties down at Jimmy's Tavern. "

"Fuck you!"

I grabbed the whole loaf of bread, a butter knife, and some raspberry jam. Then I walked out to Grampa's garage. It did smell a bit like gasoline, but it wasn't that bad.

"Grampa. Can I come and eat with you?"

"Oh, you've brought some food."

"Bread and jam. Are you hungry?"

"Hmm," he said, and nodded. I went to his small kitchenette and found some peanut butter in the cupboard. I made us up some sandwiches, and took some chilled water out of the half-fridge he had. He also had a hot-plate, but the only thing I knew how to cook was boiled hot dogs, and there weren't any in the fridge.

We sat on his old sofa and ate off of the coffee table. The peanut butter tasted old and stale, but we ate it anyway. Grampa took a long time eating, taking careful bites with his false teeth and chewing slowly, as if he expected there to be rocks in his sandwich or something.

I slept on Grampa's sofa that night. The cushions were soft, but had rough embroidery on them which scratched my face when I turned over. In the morning, Dad came in.

"Cedric?" he said, rubbing my back with his large, warm hands.

I opened my eyes, and saw him sitting on the edge of the sofa. He hadn't shaved.

"I came out last night, after your mother had gone to bed. You were sleeping already, and I didn't want to wake you up."

I yawned, and smacked my lips a couple of times.

"You heard us arguing last night."

"Yeah."

"I don't want you to worry about it. She had just been drinking too much. She's having a rough time."

"So am I."

"Me too, I guess. It'll be all right. We just have to hold onto each other. We can rely on each other. We're a family here, and we can get through this."

"Dad. I still hurt. It hasn't gone away yet. I still think about him all the time. I wanted to pull him out of the way..."

"Cedric..." he said, and held me tightly. I was crying, sputtering out my words.

"I couldn't help him. I thought..."

"You did what you could. Aw, Cedric, you did fine. There's just some things you can't help. No one could have helped him. You saw all the doctors and police trying to save him, and they couldn't. We have to let him go."

"I'm scared."

"We're all scared, but we have to face those fears. We have to let them know that we're bigger than they are. We can get through this."

We didn't say anything more. He held me for a long time, and his flannel shirt soaked up my tears. Grampa came into the living room, and sat down in his chair. He looked at us sympathetically, but I'm sure he didn't know who we were.

Friday came, and I was happy to have the week over with. We had a science test on reptiles, but I missed the first half, so I didn't know some of the questions. I thought I should have been able to skip the test, but Mrs. Cohen said that I had enough time to catch up. I didn't study in my spare time though. I had too much to think about.

After school Wayne and I went over to Colin's house. Colin had an air-hockey table. Colin's father worked in the oil fields, so he was rich. His mother always complained about late payments, but Colin still had cool toys. Wayne and Colin played air-hockey, and a raced his remote-control dune buggy around the basement. There was even a ramp for it to jump.

When we walked home, I had to pass by the cemetery again. I said good-bye to Wayne, who offered to walk me part-way home, but I said no.

It was almost eight o'clock, so the sun had gone down and the sky was already a dark blue, turning black. Inside the cemetery, the wind whipped around the tombstones. I thought I heard someone crying.

I was about to run by it, when I stopped. I didn't want anything to think they were bigger than I was. I walked into the cemetery, and over to Oliver's grave. The wind was loud, and autumn leaves rustled and flew in the wind.

Something moved on the other side of the cemetery.

"Who's there?" I called out. I don't know where I got the courage from. There was a rustling noise, and then I swear I heard a sob.

"Who's there?"

"Cedric," a voice said, totally clear.

"Y...yes?" I said. I stumbled back, and almost stepped on Oliver's grave.

"Cedric. You can hear us?"

I didn't answer. I was too scared. Then on the other side of the cemetery two forms appeared. They were dark outlines of people. Another form appeared, and another. I backed up, and hid behind Oliver's tombstone.

"Keep away."

"Cedric. We won't hurt you. We couldn't if we tried. It's me, Cedric. Emma. Auntie Emma."

I turned around, and raced for the white fence. Quickly I slipped through it, and ran home without looking back. I didn't know what to do. Auntie Emma was dead. Cancer. Years ago. Should I tell my father? Should I tell Uncle Jack? I didn't know what to do.

When I got home Dad was in the den.

"Hey Dad. What 'cha doing?"

"Trying to get these numbers right for the grainery. Something's out of order here. I can't figure it out. The numbers just don't match up. See this here?" He showed me a list of about a hundred numbers, all of them four or five digits long. "These should all match up with the numbers printed up by the computer, but they don't. They're close, but not exact." He looked at me, and put the book down. "Have you eaten?"

"No, Dad."

"Go get your Grandfather and bring him in. I'll make us up some bacon and eggs."

"Where's Mom?"

"She's asleep. She was throwing up all day. That's what happens when you drink too much. Remember that."

I went and got Grampa. I checked to make sure that he had taken his medicine, and brought him into the house. He seemed happy to be in the house, like a dog who is suddenly allowed up on the furniture.

"What did you do today, Grampa?" I asked. He just smiled and looked at me.

"You must have had a good day at school. What did you learn?"

"I don't know, Grampa. Stuff. Math and stuff."

"You should learn your lessons well, Cedric. School is important. When I was in school, my father made me stay home and work during the spring at the fall, so I only got to go to school in the winter."

Dad brought out supper. Each plate had two eggs, three pieces of bacon, and a slice of buttered toast cut in half diagonally. I noticed that they were all arranged exactly the same. I dug my toast into the yellow middle bit, and scooped it up. Grampa ate slowly, like normal.

Saturday was street hockey day. I gathered up Colin's toys, and brought them back to him. They were really fun to have, but he had been checking to see if I brought them to school every day of the week, so I knew the lending time was over.

We went to the tarmac and met up with everyone else. James and Simon had their cousins in town from the city, an older kid named Stephen and a kid our age, who had a weird name. Kimin or something. Their father was from India, James told me. He told me their father was a Paki.

We took Kimin, or whatever his name was, who turned out to be really good. He was fast on his feet, although his stick-handling sucked. He didn't score any goals, but he had five assists, and no one else had any. Stephen tried to use his size against us, keeping the puck, the dog's hamburger toy, on his stick while he charged down the middle, tossing us aside. I knew better. I just hit the back of his stick, and ran off with the puck. He was big, but slow. He shoulder-checked Bobby Chonter to the ground and made him cry. I liked Kimin, or whoever he was, but Stephen was a bully.

Cindy Perks got two goals, which was great, but we still won by two goals. The other goal was scored by Colin, but Wayne was defending against him the whole game, so he couldn't get a shot on net.

I looked up at the cemetery. It was empty. I tried to keep my attention on the game, and managed to concentrate until the game was almost over. Then I kept looking up, just making sure it remained empty.

That night Mom was drinking again. I was getting used to it. She was crying at the kitchen table, the smell of alcohol in the air. I sneaked by her, and looked into the den. Dad was sulking over the grainery book, looking from the printout to the book, and back. He had his pencil over his ear, and his flannel shirt was rolled up to his elbows.

I walked back into the kitchen, and started making myself a baloney sandwich. Mom watched me carefully the whole time. I looked up at her, and watched her eyes on me. They were dark, and her gaze felt like it went right down inside of me, burning into my belly. I finally couldn't take in anymore.

"What?" I said. My voice was higher pitched and louder than I had expected it to be.

Mom just stared at me, and pushed her eyebrows closer together. She said nothing, but I could hear her expression.

"You should have saved him."

I trembled, and my sandwich fell onto the floor. I couldn't think. I just ran out of the house, socks and all. I ran down the block, and up the hill. Before long, I found myself in the schoolyard.

I was angry, crying. I went to the cemetery. For some reason, I wasn't scared of whatever what up there, Auntie Emma or not. I wanted to talk to Oliver. I walked directly for his grave.

"Oliver!" I called down into the dirt. "I..." Suddenly there was nothing to say. I just stood there, calling into the dirt.

"He won't come up," a voice said behind me. Auntie Emma's voice. I whirled around.

"Keep back."

"Cedric. He won't come up. He won't talk. He needs help." Auntie Emma stood there, all pale and clear, wearing a hospital gown. Her eyes were sunken, and her feet were blurry. It looked as if she was slightly glowing, but the glow didn't illuminate the ground or anything, just her. Her hands looked bony and cold.

"No, keep away from me."

"Cedric, talk to me. What are you afraid of?"

"You're dead. You're a monster..."

"I am dead. I'm not a monster." I was hyperventilating.

"What do you want from me?" I seem to remember reading a book somewhere that said if you ask a ghost a question, it has to tell you the truth. It can lie to you if it just says stuff, but it can't lie to a question.

"I want you to help Oliver."

I stood there, shivering in my sock feet.

"Are you Auntie Emma?" I asked. She smiled a strange, unfamiliar smile.

"Yes. I died of Cancer. You remember. You were just a child."

"I remember."

"The others want to come out. The other people here."

"No, don't let them. Make them stay away."

"All right, all right," she said, her voice was calming. I trusted her, although I don't know why. "Listen. I need you to help me. Talk to Oliver."

"I don't know what to say."

"He hides in his coffin all day. He won't talk to anyone, or stop crying. It's been too long. He has to start healing."

"But he's dead..."

"Talk to him."

I looked around. There wasn't anyone around, and it was dark enough out that I wouldn't look crazy, so I leaned down.

"Oliver? Are you ok?"

"Cedric. Tell him to come up."

"Oliver... come up here. I want to talk." I was getting scared. What if he came up all bloody and smashed up? What if he looked like he just got hit by that truck? I heard something... Oliver... sobbing inside the grave. I put my ear to the dirt, and listened. He stopped.

"Ask him again."

"Oliver. Come on up. I want to play a game with you. Please?" I asked. Again, I heard him crying in the ground, but he wouldn't come up.

"Yes, Oliver. Come up," Auntie Emma said. She looked down at the ground, hopeful.

"Why don't you just go down and get him?"

"Cedric, it just doesn't work that way."

We stood there silent for a minute, and then I shifted around on me feet. I was scared she wanted to keep me there.

"I have to go home now."

"Come back soon. Oliver needs your help."

I walked away, but she didn't try to stop me. I felt more comfortable knowing that I could come and go as I wanted. Just as I was outside of the fence, I heard Auntie Emma's voice again.

"Cedric?"

"Yeah?"

"Could you tell Jack... tell him I still love him?"

"All right," I said. I couldn't say no.

I went to Grampa's garage, and he was reading Zane Grey.

"Hi Grampa," I said. He didn't know me.

"Oh, hello."

"How are you doing on the book?" I asked. He showed it to me, and he was halfway through.

"Good," he said, his wrinkled smile so warm.

"Grampa, you got past the first few pages." I was astonished. The only thing I ever saw him read was that Reader's Digest, and he always seemed to be on the same page.

"Mm-hmm." Grampa went back to reading. I opened his fridge, and found a half-a-can of cold stew that still looked good. I grabbed a spoon, and started into it. I should have warmed it up, but it was so good tasting that I didn't even care. I hadn't been eating enough.

I was going to sleep on Grampa's sofa again that night, but Dad came in.

"Cedric?"

I looked up. I was nearly asleep, fully dressed.

"Yeah Dad?"

"Come back to the house. Everything is all right."

I got up, and followed him into the house. He helped me get undressed, which he hadn't done since I was a child, and tucked me into bed. My own bed felt warm and comfortable, much better than the sofa.

"Cedric, you're safe here. You know that, don't you? Neither your mother nor I would ever hurt you. We're arguing, but you're always safe."

"I know, Dad," I said. I was too tired to talk, so I rolled over and fell asleep. I don't remember Dad leaving the room.

In the morning he woke me up.

"Come on, Cedric, you and I are going to church."

"Yup," I groaned. I hated church. Why couldn't I just sleep in two days a week? That's not asking too much. I got up and put on my church outfit, which consisted of my rugby pants and a white shirt. It was better than some of the other kids who had to wear ties.

Dad had made pancakes for breakfast, and I ate four of them with lots of butter and syrup. Then we walked out to the car. Mom wasn't with us.

"Isn't Mom coming to church?" I asked. Dad didn't say anything for a while. He started the car, and we drove down the block.

"No. She's hung-over. I couldn't get her up." His lips were tight together, and he stuck out his bottom jaw for a moment.

"Will she go to the later service?" I asked. Really, I didn't care that much, because I didn't like church, but Mom never missed it, except the Sunday after Oliver died, and I guess the couple of weeks since.

"No. Probably not. She needs her rest." He didn't say anything else the whole ride there. We parked, and went into the church. Dad talked politely with a few people. Colin and his mom were there, so I went over to him. Wayne didn't have to go to church. He was lucky.

"Hi Colin," I said. Colin's mom was talking to Mr. Zolinski, a thin, good-looking farmer. Mr. Zolinski had the fanciest truck in town.

"Hi Cedric. Good game yesterday," he said, "that goal you scored was a good one."

"Yeah, I would have done better but that big guy kept trying to knock me over, so I always passed it to Cindy. He wouldn't have knocked over Cindy."

"Yeah, if he did, she'd knock him on his ass!" he said. Then we both looked around quickly to see if anyone had heard him. Luckily, no one did.

The priest came out, so everyone shut up. I hustled over to my Dad, who was sitting down already.

The priest started talking. We were sitting beside Margerie Canwell, and I couldn't even see the marks were Mom had slapped her. I guess Mom didn't actually dig her fingernails in, like I thought she did. She smelt like perfume, kind of a peach smell. I thought that maybe after the sermon I would ask her if Mom hurt her, maybe try to apologize or something.

Everyone said "Amen," and I quickly paid attention. The next time everyone said "Amen," I managed to mumble it along. I thought about talking to the priest. Maybe he would know about ghosts and things, but I don't remember him ever saying anything about them. He always just said that we would either go to Heaven or Hell, not hang around the cemetery. I had heard something about Purgatory, but I didn't know what that was.

Mr. and Mrs. Collichuk were there, but Darren wasn't. He was still in jail, I guessed. Usually the Collichuks sat in the front row, all proud to be so holy, and made sure to look around before dropping a load of bills into the collection box. Now they sat at the back, away from everyone else.

I looked over to Colin, and could see him wriggling in his seat. His mom whispered to him, and he sat still, sullenly. I laughed to myself.

The priest continued, talking about the father, son, and Holy Ghost. That caught my attention, because he said "ghost." I thought that maybe there was a Heaven, Hell, Purgatory-whatever that is -and a ghost world. I was being hopeful.

After service, we went home. Dad told me to check on Grampa, to make sure that he took his morning medicine.

I walked into the garage, and quickly noticed that Grampa's bicycle was gone. I raced into his bedroom, but he wasn't there either. Grampa had gone traveling again.

I ran to the house, and told Dad.

"Aw Christ, I knew he would do this again. Quickly get changed and get back down here."

I ran up the stairs while taking my shirt off, and slipped my pants off as I hopped into my room. My jeans were on the floor, and I pulled a T-shirt off of a coat hanger. I ran downstairs again, and put on my runners. Dad was ready as well. We both walked quickly out to the car.

"He's probably at the old lot," I said. Dad nodded, and we drove over there. Grampa was nowhere to be seen, so Dad went and talked to George Dillman.

"Hello George," Dad said, "looks like Judy's father has rode off on his bicycle again. Seen him?"

"Nope, 'fraid I haven't. Been out here all morning pulling in the garden, and he hasn't been here."

"Do you think you could give me a call if you see him?"

"Sure."

"Thanks George."

We drove around the streets for a while, checking the sidewalks and front lawns. Sometimes Grampa would fall over, and just lay there waiting for someone to come pick him up. We spotted his bicycle over by the ice cream shop.

We walked in, and Grampa was sitting at a booth, wearing a hockey helmet, and eating a soft ice-cream cone.

"Hi Grampa!" I said. I was excited to see him.

"Oh... hello," he said calmly. He had ice-cream all over his chin. Dad went up and talked to the Jenni Rudd, who was working behind the register. A few moments later Dad came back with two soft ice-cream cones. The good kind, with half chocolate half vanilla. He sat down, and gave me one.

"Hello Eli," he said. Grampa looked up at him, and kept eating. "You know you're not supposed to go bike riding alone. We didn't know where you were." Dad's voice was soft and kind. He was frustrated, but knew that Grampa couldn't be blamed.

"This is good," Grampa said, holding up his ice cream. It was good. We never got ice cream after church. Dad ate his ice cream quietly after that, staring out the window at the cars going by.

We threw Grampa's bike into the back of the station wagon, but we had to push the seats forward to do it, and I had to sit with the bike, while Grampa got the passenger seat.

Back at home, Mom had gotten up and made herself some oatmeal. We came in and she was sitting in the living room, watching TV and eating the oatmeal right from the pot. Dad moaned loudly, and went to the den. Grampa was back in his garage, Dad in his den, and I didn't know where to be. So, I sat on the floor and watched TV. Mom was watching some show that was trying to sell cleaning fluid. They dumped mud and paint and grease onto a kitchen floor, and then mopped it up. It was really boring.

I ended up walking down to Brown River. I sat down and chucked rocks into the current, trying to make the biggest 'ker-plunk.' Cindy Perks, and her friend Janice walked across the bridge, so I yelled up at them.

"Hey, Cindy!"

"Cedric?" she said, "wait a sec." They both came down. Janice was wearing a down-filled jacket, even though it wasn't that cold. "What are you doing down here?"

"Nothing," I said, "just hanging out. What are you doing?"

"Going for a walk. Thought we would check out Mount Sutton."

"That's way too far to walk," I said. It was a full day walk to get up it. It wasn't very big, and hardly worthy of being called a mountain, but it was the biggest hill around, and it did have some nice cliffs on the far side.

"We were just going to look at it," Janice said, then stared down into the water.

"Mind if I come along?" I asked.

After we got back, it was already getting late. We climbed about halfway up before we decided to go back. We saw a couple of deer, and watched a beaver swimming around the creek over by Baby Flynn's house. Baby Flynn is the fattest man in Spirit Grove, but he's nice. Everyone likes Baby.

I was feeling relaxed walking home. Cindy and Janice were laughing at my jokes, and we talked about hockey strategies for the next street hockey game, which made Janice bored. Cindy and I made up secret code words for specific plays, so that we would know what to do without everyone else getting in on the plan.

They turned off down Pioneer Street, and I kept walking home. I didn't really want to go, but there was nowhere else to go, and it was late.

When I got there, Mom and Dad were arguing again.

"He could have been anywhere? He could have fallen down and hurt himself, and you don't even care!" my Dad yelled. He was really mad.

"I told him I wouldn't put him in a home. I told him. You think I'm going to break my word? No fucking way."

"Look here, you stop drinking already. I've put up with it this long, but no more. You straighten up. I'm not going to be married to some fucking drunk like Donna Swirski, drunk out of her mind in Jimmy's, sucking cock for a bottle of vodka. That's what happens, you know. That's what happens to drunks around here!"

"Fuck you! Don't you dare tell me how to live! Just hide in your little den there. You didn't give birth to him. I did! He was part of me!"

"Judy... he was my son too." Dad's voice was sad and defeated when he said this, and he walked away to his den.

I went up to my room, and didn't come out. I didn't eat supper, again.

Monday morning came quickly. I was still tired when my clock went off. I had it set to the country station, so I would get up to turn it off quickly. I dressed quickly, in my jeans and striped shirt, and went downstairs.

Dad had already gone to work. He had left early. I guess he still hadn't figured out his problem yet. Mom was still asleep, so I made toast and jam.

School was all right. We played volleyball in gym class, and our team won. Colin and I were on the same team, and we were unbeatable. We always bumped it to each other and away from Simon Drake because he's way too squat to play well. Simon was frustrated.

After school, everyone had to go home early, so we didn't get to play street hockey. Colin's mom was having dinner with Mr. Zolinski, and she wanted Colin home for it. I'd have thought that she would want to get rid of Colin so she could be alone with Mr. Zolinski, but I guess she wanted the two of them to get aquatinted. He seemed nice enough in church. Colin didn't like him.

So I went home, and hung out with Grampa. I spent all evening there. I even did some homework on his coffee table. Mom came over with macaroni and cheese for the both of us. She said she expected a tip, but I don't really know what she was getting at.

That night I went back to the cemetery. It sounds crazy, but I just had to go. I was still scared, but I took a warm jacket, and it wasn't as bad as before.

"Auntie Emma?" I called. There was no response, so I called again a few times.

"Cedric," she called, and rose up from the ground. I was suddenly scared again, "thank you for coming back."

"Yeah."

"Oliver is the same. Still won't come up. I'm afraid for him."

"What happens if he doesn't come up? Will he die down there?"

"Cedric, he is already dead. He won't die again, but he can be very unhappy for a very long time, and I don't want to see that."

Another form appeared out from the ground. I jumped back.

"Who's that?" I called out.

"Cedric, that's Louis Stannard. He's from England. Don't worry, he's nice. He's a nice man."

I stared at him, and the form waved at me. I smiled, and he floated over. I clenched my teeth, but didn't run away.

"Hello, young man. Sorry to see your troubles," he said. He had an English accent, like channel thirteen at nighttime.

"Thanks," I said. I was shivering again.

"So young. They should string that man up who killed him."

"Oh, don't talk like that," Auntie Emma said to him.

"I knew this one had the gift. Madeline said so."

"Gift?" I asked.

"Madeline Crinny," Auntie Emma said, "third from the left in the front row, said right at the funeral that you had the gift. The ability to see us. Madeline was a medium during her lifetime. Told fortunes, the future, talked to spirits, read tea leaves."

"Auntie Emma," I asked, "what are you doing here? Aren't you supposed to go to Heaven?"

"I don't know where I'm supposed to go. I can feel that there is somewhere, but I'm not ready. I'm waiting."

"For what?"

"Jack. He has a plot right beside me. I'm waiting for him."

I thought about it for a while, and felt a little sick. She was waiting for Uncle Jack to die. I didn't know what to think about it. So instead, I just changed the topic.

"I want to talk to Oliver," I said, "alone, if you please." They both nodded, and sunk back into the ground. Seeing them wasn't so bad, but knowing that they could pop up underneath me was really scary. I walked over to Oliver's grave, and called down into the dirt.

"Oliver? Are you ready to come up yet?"

Nothing. Just a few sobs. Didn't he ever get over it?

"Come on, Oliver. I think Scooby-Doo is on TV. Don't you want to come and watch with me?"

It didn't work. I put my mouth right to the ground.

"Oliver! What's the matter?"

"Mommy..."

I heard it. He spoke, and it was his voice. Suddenly I imagined him popping up through the ground with my face in the dirt, and jumped back.

"Auntie Emma?"

She rose up from the ground, silently.

"I'm going home. I'll be back tomorrow. We'll try again."

I didn't go back the next day. In fact, I didn't return until three days after. It snowed, and got really cold. I should've gone out then, I can see that now, but at the time it was just getting to be too much of a burden. Maybe I'm selfish.

Mom and Dad continued fighting. She was drinking more and more, and Dad wasn't helping at all. He was going out all the time, or ignoring her, or arguing. After supper one day and they started yelling at each other, loudly, and didn't even stop when I came into the room.

"You're a drunk! I can see that now, only it's too late! You're pathetic," my Dad yelled. I had never heard him be so attacking. Normally he was defensive.

"I may be a drunk, but you're a useless wimp of a man. You going to live your life running away? You have this problem as much as I do. You can't even face that your son is dead."

"He's dead! He's dead and has been for a long time now. I'm not running away from it, I'm dealing with it as best that I can... and you're one to talk about running away from it!"

"You fucking bastard!" Mom yelled, and slapped the side of his head with her fist. Dad stumbled, and backed away.

"I can't speak to you. I don't even know who you are."

Mom collapsed on the sofa, crying. I didn't go to help her. I left for the graveyard.

It was an icy walk, with the steep hill right by the school. I almost slipped twice, but managed to keep my balance by whirling my arms around my head. It didn't look very cool, so I hope no one was watching.

The ghosts were up, watching. They were whirling around, looking like frosty angels in the falling snow. I worried about them for a moment, because it didn't look like they were dressed for the weather, but then, maybe they don't feel cold? I don't know.

Aunt Emma was there, smiling.

"Isn't it wonderful?" she asked me.

"Yeah, sure is."

"I always loved winter. The early months anyway, before January. After January it usually started to get me down, but these early snows..."

"Hockey season is almost here. The lake is almost ready for skating."

"Oh yes, of course. Hockey is your sport, isn't it."

"Yup."

"How is Jack doing?"

"He's fine, I guess. I haven't heard from him for a while. He stopped coming around when Mom started harassing him. Mom isn't doing so well."

"Oh. Well, I guess you'd like to talk to Oliver then."

I walked over to Oliver's grave, and crouched down. I swept some of the snow off of the tombstone, and put a handprint on the grave.

"Oliver, it's me. I'd like to talk to you."

Nothing.

"Oliver, please, come up and talk to me. I need to speak to you... about Mom and Dad, and the accident, and... everything."

Still nothing. I thought I heard him crying, but it was windy, and the wind buffeted my ears which made it hard to hear.

"Oliver... please..." I started to cry, again. "I don't want to be at home. I want to be here. With you."

I stood up and walked quickly out of the graveyard. Aunt Emma had seen me cry enough times. I was embarrassed.

Walking home was pretty cold, but I was getting used to being outside all of the time, so it wasn't so bad. I was walking away from the graveyard, and I still had tears in my eyes. I saw a couple of adults walking towards me, so I quickly wiped them off of my face. You could still tell I had been crying. I felt like a big baby.

The couple were holding hands, and talking, laughing a little as they got closer. They seemed happy enough, but when I got closer, I realized that it was Mr. and Mrs. Collichuk. I looked up at them, and they fell silent and looked into my eyes. They could tell I had been crying. We passed by each other without saying anything, and they walked away in silence.

It took me a while to get home, because I took the long way to help clear my eyes. When I got home, I went right up to my room. Mom was passed out in the living room. I quickly got undressed and hopped into bed. It was really cold, and I shivered beneath my down quilt. Soon the warmth crept in, and my legs relaxed. Dad came into my room.

"Cedric?" Dad said.

"Yeah," I answered, rolling over and rubbing my eyes as if I had been asleep for a while.

"Just got in, didn't you."

"Yeah."

"I guess your mother and I scared you with our fighting. I'm not mad at you for leaving." I was relieved when he said this. I thought I was in trouble for being out so late on a school night.

"I needed some room."

"I know. I know. Cedric, you know I love you, don't you?"

"Uh, yeah Dad." How embarrassing.

"Don't think I don't love you, because I do, and I always will, no matter what happens between your mother and I. Cedric, I need some room, too, from your mother, from this house, from everything. I need to get away from everything and think things over. I'm still hurting, from Oliver's..."

"Me too, Dad."

"...and I can't get better with your mother..." he started sniffling, and his lips became puffy with sadness, "...and I can't help her... I tried, Cedric... I really did... but I can't..." Dad lay down beside me and held me closely. He was warm and sad, and it felt good to have him near me. I started crying too, again. It seemed like since Oliver's death I cried twice a day.

"Dad, when will you be back?"

"I don't know."

"Take me with you, please. I can't stay here with her either."

In the morning Dad was gone, and I wasn't. I dressed quickly and raced out of the house. It was one of those mornings when I wished that I had a big oak tree outside my window I could crawl down. Since I didn't, the quick run was the best plan. I had my school books in my backpack, and my baseball cap on, so I ran down the stairs and out the door. My shoes made heavy thuds on the ground, but Mom didn't catch me. I don't know if she slept in her bedroom or the living room, or anywhere else for the matter. I had gotten out clean.

Mrs. Cohen wasn't in her normal, understanding mood that morning; I don't know why. She found out I didn't do any of my homework, and made me sit at the front of the class, right in front of her desk. Maybe she thought getting me away from my friends would motivate me to do my homework or something. She was wrong, obviously. I did my schoolwork though, I mean, it's difficult to slack off when you can feel the teacher's breath on you. Needless to say, it was another bad day at school.

After school I stuck around with Wayne and Colin, playing hockey. I had forgotten to bring my stick, so Wayne let me use his, only he was left-handed, so his stick was curved the wrong way. I couldn't aim a shot for the life of me, but it was still fun, and we played until it was dark.

"Hey Cedric, you want to go to the lake tonight? We can play hockey there, on the real ice and everything. I can lend you a stick," Colin said.

"Yeah!" I yelled, overenthusiastic. I didn't only mean hockey, it meant an excuse not to be at home. "Wayne? You in?"

"Of course!" he said, "but you'll have to call me after supper, in case my parents say no."

"Yeah. Hey, Cedric, you want to eat at my house."

This was another stroke of luck for me. "Great!"

We walked to his house, and his mother agreed to feed me supper. She made fried chicken and boiled some perogys, the kind with cottage cheese in the middle.

"So, Cedric, how are your parents doing?"

"They're still upset about Oliver's death."

Colin's mother jolted up, and looked at me sympathetically.

"Oh, of course. I'm really sorry."

"That's all right. Mom is still really upset, and Dad..." I stopped. My father was gone, and I didn't know if he was coming back. I lost my father. I took a bite of chicken, and chewed without tasting. Maybe Dad went to Great Plains and found a new family, and didn't want us anymore. Maybe he didn't love me.

I didn't realize I had started crying, and my nose started to run. I quickly regained my senses, and ran upstairs to the bathroom. I cried for a long time, but then washed my face and came back down. They were just finishing up and taking their dishes away, so I quickly stuffed a couple of perogys into my mouth. The house was very silent.

I called home, to tell Mom I was going to the lake, but there was no answer.

The lake was frozen over, and Dennis Gardner had cleared a large patch of ice with his snow blower. He had one of those snow blowers that you can ride, so if the ice was thick enough to support that thing, it was thick enough to support us. Some people were already on in. A few adults were skating around, and some older kids had set up a net. They let us play with them, because they knew we were good. Wayne finally showed up, and joined up too. Wayne was late because his mother made lasagna. Wayne was on the other team, because Colin and I never got to play on the same team. They still won though, because they had the good older kids, but they didn't win by much, and I scored three goals, more than anyone all night. Colin didn't score any, but he had a couple of assists.

Colin's mom dropped me off at home. The lights were on, so I came in quietly. Mom was drunk, and Dad was still gone. I hid upstairs in my room until it was time to sleep. Mom didn't even know I was home. She didn't even care.

It was about a week later, which is tonight, when Grampa acted up again. He had been pretty obedient, staying in the garage. I took him to the Q-Mart to buy Rolaids once, so it isn't like he never got out.

Mom had been drinking and hanging around at Jimmy's Tavern, and I was kept getting in trouble at school because I didn't have enough time to do my homework, so I had gotten detention three times that week.

Grampa got it in his head to go out for a walk in the winter snow. It wasn't all that cold out, but he didn't bring his good jacket, just his cardigan and a scarf. He went out alone.

I found out because George Dillman called asking for my father. When I said that Dad wasn't home, he said that Grampa was in front of the empty lot again, yelling about someone stealing his home. Mom wasn't home, so I had to go get him.

It was already dark out, so I brought my flashlight. I didn't know that he didn't have a good jacket on.

Grampa was in a state. He was all yelling, and blue-lipped from the cold. Mr. Dillman was out there too, with a cup of steaming liquid, but Grampa was having nothing to do with him.

"I tried to give him a blanket," George told me, "but he threw it on the ground. I don't like having people treat my gifts like that."

"Sorry Mr. Dillman. You know my Grampa. He's just like that," I said, trying to apologize. Mr. Dillman was a nice guy, but too cranky. "Come on Grampa," I said, grabbing his cold hand.

"Oh, I'm sorry, who are you?"

"Cedric, your Grandson. Remember? Look, Grampa, we have to take you home and give you your medicine."

"I don't know where my home is. Someone stole it."

"Just come with me, Grampa, and we'll go somewhere nice and warm." He shuffled along with me. About half-way, I took off my jacket, and gave it to him. He looked ridiculous in it, but at least he was warmer. I was cold, and the batteries died on my flashlight.

When we finally got home, Mom was inside the house, so we went to Grampa's garage. That's when we hit the patch of ice. I didn't see it, and Grampa slipped and his head went smack on the pavement.

I thought he was dead. I thought that he was killed by the blow. I screamed. Mom ran out, wearing her robe and carrying a half-empty bottle of rum, and ran to his side. She stunk of alcohol.

"Dad!" she called out. Grampa shook his head, and opened his eyes.

"Ouch," he said. I started to laugh. Grampa wasn't dead at all. He even smiled at Mom.

"Dad, are you all right?"

"I'm sorry. I don't believe we've met."

"God dammit, Dad, I'm Judy, your daughter."

"Oh..." he said, and started drifting off.

"Dad, what were you doing out there," Mom said. Her voice was harsh, and I could tell she was really mad at him.

"I was going home." Grampa sat up.

"Your home is here." Mom took a drink from the bottle of rum in desperation.

"Oh..."

"Mom," I said. "He's got blood on his head." Mom looked, and his grey hair was sticking together with the dark liquid. Mom started to cry.

"I can't take this. I can't take anymore." Her body shuddered, and she put her head down onto the frozen pavement. I just looked at her. She stunk of alcohol, and hadn't combed her hair in a long time.

"Get into the car," Mom said, "and get your Grampa in. He's not staying here anymore."

"What?"

"We're putting him into a home."

"No, Mom, we can't!"

"Do as you're told, Oliver... I mean Cedric." That really got me, so I didn't argue anymore. I put Grampa into the backseat, and I sat in the front. Mom got in and started it up, so I turned the heat up full, for Grampa's sake, and my own.

"It's like taking care of two little children," Mom said, her voice harsh and angry, "I can't spend my life taking care of you. You walk away without caring, you leave whenever you want to, you drove my husband away!" She was yelling at Grampa, but he didn't appear to notice. Mom backed out of the driveway, and started driving down the street to the highway. "You don't realize how lucky you are. I argued for you so much. My husband said I had to let you go to that home, but I told you... I promised you I wouldn't..." Tears started streaming down her face again. "I can't care for you anymore. I can't spend my life caring for you every day. I can't..."

We sped down the highway, and Mom was swerving. She was drunk, and crying didn't help.

"You've been such a burden on me for so long, you haven't been yourself, just a memory of... of the father I loved. I have to let...

That's when the doe ran out in front of the car. It happened so fast. Mom tried to swerve, couldn't do it fast enough, and the front of the car took the doe's legs out from under her, and her light body smashed the windshield. The car lurched around, and I bonked my head on the dash. Mom hit the steering wheel, and the horn honked. The doe bounced off, legs still flailing as if she were trying to run, and came to rest on the pavement as we squealed to a stop.

Now we're stopped here, and Mom is on the road, wearing that ratty robe. The doe has stopped fighting, and is just lying there, dead. Mom is crying.

Then she kneels down beside the doe, and wraps her arms around it. She lets out a loud scream, a wail, and her body shudders again and again. Her face is right in the bloody flesh. Then, I can see that through the broken bones, through the pavement scraped flesh and bloody fur, Oliver's translucent arms reaching up, and around Mom's trembling shoulders.

A Carnival in Dry Lands

I heard the train roll into town at noon. I noticed because usually we only had a train at dawn and one at dusk, but never at noon.

Claudette had put out some bread and butter for lunch. It hadn't rained for over two months, so the garden was only spitting up small, dried vegetables, which we saved for our suppers. Claudette was a beautiful woman. She had thin dark hair and a wide face; the kind of face you don't see anymore. She was also a good wife, but she immersed herself too deeply into her religion after our daughter died. Lily was born too soon, and only lived two weeks.

"Preacher Harmony looks like he needs a break from the heat," she said.

"Don't we all," I said, peeling off my shirt, and exposing my dark tanned chest, and the burn scars up and down my arms, "if we don't get a break from it, we'll blow away like dust in the fields."

"Well, just pray for rain. I'm sure God will grant, if it's in His plans for us."

"I'm sick of praying to God, and He hasn't delivered any rain yet. If He does plan on keeping us alive, He'd better damn well hurry up or all He'll find is husks of skin sitting on kitchen chairs or face down in the dirt. I'm going out to the forge. Maybe I can get something done and bring us in some money."

"This is the Lord's day, Emery, you really shouldn't..."

"If I don't, then our good Lord is going to have two less worshippers down here to celebrate His grandness." I ran my hand across my chin, and felt the three weeks beard growth since I had stopped shaving. It wasn't important enough to waste the water on, and I hated shaving dry.

I put a half a piece of dry bread into my mouth and walked out the screen door. I looked around the forge. No one in town had any money, so there was nothing coming in, and the fields were too dry to grow anything. I had all my tools and the forge, but nothing to make. Work had been good last year, and even better the year before, but not this one, and the money never did last from one year to the next.

My dog, Smoky, looked up at me from the shade. She had a sadness about her because we couldn't feed her. She kept herself alive on field mice, gophers, and the occasional rabbit.

I sat down next to the anvil and rolled myself a cigarette. Before I finished, I rested my sweaty head in my hands.

*   *   *

Down the hill we could see where the train stopped, and there was a gathering of people around it. I couldn't see exactly what they were doing, so I went down to find out, and Smoky followed behind.

It was on Murray Sigurdson's fields. Murray was standing in the middle of the group pretending to direct all the others, while they mostly ignored him. It wasn't that unusual, as everyone tended to ignore Murray, and Murray always wanted to be in control of everything.

"Hey Murray, what's all this?"

"It's a carnival. These fellahs came into town on the train, and they gave me fifty bucks to set up on this piece of land."

"Bit early in the year for the carnival, isn't it?"

"I figured so, but seeing as no one can do any work until it rains, these guys might make some money here, and maybe I can get a cut of it."

"No one in town's got any money."

"They'll find some. Once they hear a good time going on, they'll dig up some money from somewhere."

I walked around for a while, and then a big guy wearing a leopard skin came up to me and said I could do all my looking when it was ready.

*   *   *

Claudette was ecstatic when I told her about it. She hadn't been to a carnival since she left Quebec. I told her it was a waste of time and money, but she didn't see it that way.

After a dinner of new potatoes and some small carrots, I told her we could spend a couple of hours at the carnival, unless it rained and we had work to do. I even pulled out a few dollars I was saving for either a special occasion or if I ran out of tobacco, and gave it to her.

*   *   *

The merry-go-round had horses of every kind you could imagine. It had palominos and dapple greys, grown horses and ponies. It kicked up so much dust that you had to practically get close enough to ride it just to see what it was. Claudette went for a few rounds, but I just stood back watching her. She looked so happy. I hadn't seen her that happy since our wedding. She was wearing a thin brown dress that blew softly as she stretched to grab a brass ring. She never managed to grab one, but she managed to hold on tight enough to keep from being thrown to the ground.

There were tents of all sorts put up; each one with a man out front announcing some great mystery behind the flaps. One had Globbo, the world's fattest man in it. Another tent kept a woman who had the ugliest face in the world; they called her the Mule-Woman of New Mexico. Or depending on your idea of a good time, you could pay a dime and go into a tent to see a geek-boy bite the head off of a live chicken.

The Ferris wheel stood tall and impressive. It looked bigger than anything that came before it. The paint was old and the hinges rusting, but it was still the most beautiful thing in the valley. Claudette and I went on it, and we could see all the way to the town hall from the highest point. Our shack was also in view, but not the forge. I held on tightly, but my arms felt weak from the heat, and I got dizzy quickly. After we got off, I had to steady myself.

Claudette met up with a couple of other women, so they went off walking while I went into the beer tent. It wasn't much to look at, and the canvas smelled like vomit. Bill Mitchell was at the end of the bar, drinking beer and rubbing a piece of ice against his blind eye. Paul Gallichenko and his wife Janice sat at a table holding hands and talking about things too important to talk about at home. Lloyd Durand was chatting with one of the carnival workers, while a dwarf was smoking a cigar and getting hammered. I just sat at the bar.

When I came out I saw the man selling lighting rods. They were good, strong metal rods with symbols on the tops. The symbols looked like crosses with different designs on top of them, like letters of the alphabet at strange angles, or Egyptian eyes. One even looked like a horseshoe with the arch pointing upwards like they do in forges, so the luck runs down upon you.

"Come on up, young man, and buy a lightning rod. It may just save your life in case you ever get lighting raining down upon you."

"Mister," I said, "it's been sixty-seven days since we've seen a drop of rain, so I don't figure on having much trouble with lightning."

"Have you ever seen lightning without rain?"

"No."

"There you have it. All you need to do is attach this rod to your house, and within days you'll have more rain pouring down upon you than Noah did. Gather 'round everyone. Need rain? I have just the solution. Mitch Haywood's lightning attracting rods..."

I waited around for a while trying to figure out what was going on while more and more people gathered around the man. Soon most of the town was around him, giving him money. Preacher Harmony came out of the crowd.

"Please," he said to me, looking as if everyone in the crowd had forsaken him, "you're not going to unite with this pagan idolatry, are you?"

"I wasn't planning on buying one."

"Oh, thank God. At least I have one whose soul in true."

"What about Claudette?"

"Yes, her too, of course."

After the preacher disappeared, nearly defeated, into the crowd, I took a good look at the rod Gus Luchinski bought, and it didn't look all that difficult to make. I waited around until the crowd died down, and then I went over to the man.

"Say, where do you get these things?"

"I have a group of blacksmiths across the continent working hard with a variety of metals and techniques designing the best lightning attracters possible. They burn special herbs in their fires, and pound the metal moonwise while facing north to bring the most power to the creation. Here, feel the craftsmanship." I grabbed the top of one and looked at the forge weld.

"I have a forge a couple fields over," I said, "and there isn't any money coming in for anything else right now, so how about giving me a try. I could really use a break."

*   *   *

"It looks like a good job, and I don't think I'm going to get much anything else out of this town," I said, sitting at the kitchen table.

"I still don't like it. It sounds like the Devil's work. Those weird symbols can't be Christian."

"Well, seems to me working with questionable symbols in order to survive wouldn't bar us from Heaven. Anyway, they have crosses on them, just a little different, like the difference between Catholic and Protestant, only in a symbol."

"You're probably right, but what if you're not? What if it is a sin?"

"Can we afford not to risk it? We can do penance if I'm wrong."

Claudette softly put her thumb up to her lips and then ran it down her jawline. Then she looked up at me, in agreement.

"I got to get back to the carnival. They'll be closing up about now, and I need to talk to that guy about the job."

Smoky looked up from under the porch as I walked by her. She didn't follow.

*   *   *

A carnival is a strange sight when empty. All the drunks passed out in the field, and the carnies still flittering back and forth in the darkness. Large men lumber around making sure everything is safe for the night, with cigarettes hanging from the lips of their tired mouths. Women in gypsy costumes from the dancing-girl stage sneak into their lover's tents. The dwarf had sobered up, and walking with a dog larger than he was.

I went over to the canvas tent which a man directed me to. I looked for something to knock on, but as there was nothing, I just called in.

"Hello? Mister Haywood?"

"C'mon in," was the response. I walked in, and the lightning rod salesman was leaning on a rickety table counting money.

"You sure got a lot of money out of the town today. These people, they're starving, you know. They don't shell out money like that for just anything, especially something that isn't for farming."

"I don't see how a farmer can survive without an instrument to bring the rains. And even if it did rain, the lightning would track you and strike you down."

"Yeah, I suppose you're right. So how about it. Can you give me a job?"

"I'm sure I could find some work for a good blacksmith. How many rods can you make for me in three days?"

"I don't know. Maybe fifty? It depends on how tough the designs are."

"Here's something I printed up. Can you read?"

"I was taught."

"Good. There are fifteen different symbols I have patented. You can work with those. And here is a batch of my secret herb mixture, put this in the forge before you heat the metal."

"Looks like hay."

"It's a special blend of wild plants from across Africa and Asia. These herbs never fail to attract the lightning."

"Okay."

"I sell the rods for five dollars apiece, so I can only afford a dollar each for them. Otherwise I wouldn't have enough money to travel through the country selling them, or get the mystic herbs."

"Yeah, sounds fair enough."

*   *   *

The next day I started up the forge for the first time in two weeks. The heat seared though my early morning chills, and soon I took off my shirt and just wore my thick leather apron.

When the fires were hot enough, I threw in the special herbs. They flared in the heat, but soon burnt down to nothing. Then I took one of my metal rods and heated its end to a glowing red. I put it on the anvil and began hammering.

By the end of the day I had made fifteen lightning rods, using four different symbols. My arm was sore, and I had forgotten to stop to eat. I walked back to the house and dropped my filthy jeans on the front step. Claudette had dinner all ready. Potatoes and cabbage.

"I was thinking, Emery, maybe if you made a couple of the rods with just the cross on them."

"Well, I'll make a couple for Mitch, and if he doesn't like them I can always donate them to the church. I'm sure that they could use a few more crosses around."

*   *   *

The following two days I finished up the rest of the rods. I only managed to make forty, but I figured that would be enough. Five of them were holy crosses, but the rest were his symbols. The third night I went back to the carnival to give them all to Mitch.

"Very nice. Good work here. Did you follow the instructions?"

"Well, most of them anyway. Sometimes I found myself pounding the wrong way, but mostly I did it right."

"That's a minor part anyway. I'll take them all at the agreed price."

"What about the crosses? My wife thought it might be a good idea to have a little religion in them."

"Nice touch. I'm sure they'll sell to all those who are too afraid of the other symbols. You did well," he said, and counted out eight five-dollar bills and handed them to me. It was the most money I had in my hands for a long time.

"So when do you think the rains are going to come?"

"Should be here in a day or two, I suppose."

*   *   *

The carnival packed up and left heading south. I went to the general store and stored up on a few necessities. I even bought Claudette a few new knitting needles.

Every morning, behind the rods, the sky glared blue, with the sun burning brightly. The only clouds in the sky were thin white ridges, like the ribs of some starving animal.

Lemons on Venus

Written for Christophe and Susanne

She was a comma, wishing it were a period. She was a dress hanging from a clothesline on a rainy day. She was a daughter of the scientific age. A goddess with fine hair of the mousiest brown, she had strong hands and an overbite just prominent enough to be cute to friends but irritating to orthodontists. Her name was Isabelle, but she called herself Isa.

It was a Saturday when Isa first saw him. A flash of electricity shot through her when he looked at her. What was his name? What was he like? She could never tell at first. At first it was just a feeling. Intrigue. The thrill at seeing his lopsided smile turn up to greet her. And also fear this time, because something about it felt serious.

Then again, most things felt serious to Isa. She was a serious person, with a serious job.
And Isa may very well be one of the most important people on the planet. The one thing that wasn't at all serious was her love life. Being a self-conscious creature, slumped under a 5'9" frame, Isa preferred to stay at the darkest part of any room. Ideally, isolated in a lab, where she could concentrate on the successes of plant evolution instead of her own physiology. When you're concentrating on something else, it's easier to ignore people staring. Her body felt monstrously large from the inside. It felt like a giant cedar, swaying in the slightest wind. She longed to be a cherry tree, fully radiant in pink. Or an *Iris tenax*. A bonsai. Isa did her best to forget her body.
 Fortunately, she was a master of living in her mind.

Seven years ago, Isa graduated from university with distinction, honors, and an armful of awards. She'd done her Master's degree in one year instead of two, and produced a variant of asexual marigolds for her doctorate, which earned her an international science prize and a juicy cash bonus. She spent it in two years of looking for that perfect job and finding herself. She made changes. For one, she discovered a love for shooting pool late at night with her best friend, Doreen.

Then she landed it. Usuteshihu. Research division. Despite her previous successes, the importance of it shocked them both at first. As NASA's little corporate buddy, Usuteshihu had created the space station farms – things like the zero G algae and oxycacti, an epiphytic cacti which need no soil and expel twice the oxygen of regular cacti. Not enough for a human to live off, but every little bit helps in space. This was kind of job even Isa dreamed of in university. Soon it too became perfectly normal. Just another lab with higher security. And of course, the kind of place where in just under three years, she could initiate a breakthrough that would probably be entered prominently in every documented record of human history.

It's called Ironweed. Or at least that's its common name around the lab. Isa created it meticulously, searching through genetic links, swapping an A for a T here, a G for a D there. After just three years, Ironweed was her baby. It's a plant based on the thistle, except with genetic adaptations. For one, it thrives on very little atmosphere and releases vast quantities of carbon dioxide and oxygen both day and night – easily ten times the volume of any normal plant. Perfect for a planet like Mars, which lacks plate tectonics. That means there is plenty of carbon dioxide, but it isn't released into the atmosphere. Ironweed can do that. And that's just the opener.

She saw him at the library. What was Isa doing at the library? Theoretically, she was researching plants. Subconsciously, she was looking for interesting men. She would linger around the botany section, then nip over to auto mechanics or copyright law for a break. Her new project was already causing her more grief than she could deal with. There was a lot of pressure, being the hotshot at the office, the one who may well bring life to the red planet. That kind of reputation lingered, even though Ironweed peaked two years ago, and she had been off it for a year already. Of course she had protested her reassignment, but they had pulled her anyway and given her a new task. A tougher one – one that suited her better than the housekeeping that remained the Ironweed file.

Venus. Impossible.

But that's what they had said about Mars.

Her beloved Ironweed project had been given to a lesser team, one who simply monitored the probes to see how they were doing. Years one, two, and three were spent creating the plants. Year four was testing, which Isa was only partially involved with. Year five the seeds were delivered to Mars and scattered across the surface along with specially designed transmitters. Year six, there were two generations of Ironweed growing, but none had lived a full life cycle. That would occur at approximately year 15, if everything went as planned.

He was hovering around the section on ancient religions. Bad sign. She presumed this meant he was into anthropology. And that meant he was unemployed. She chastised herself for assuming the worst. People are usually more complex than plants, which makes their genetic impulses more multilayered and difficult to discern. But it's no secret that there isn't much work for anthropologists, except perhaps at universities where they train new anthropologists, which is the cruel joke universities play. While studying, students are presented with dignified professionals who have the degree they are working towards, and they're employed. They sometimes travel for work. Maybe own a house. It's only after graduation that the prank is revealed.

Isa hadn't even begun to crack Venus after a solid year. People were starting to talk. Even if it was Saturday, she couldn't hang around the hockey section all day – she had to focus. She thrived on focus. And really, what else was she going to do on a weekend. Laundry? Sit around and pet Nepeta?

Meeting people is difficult. Going up to them without an introduction, excruciating. What do you say? 'Hi, you look kinda nice and your smile just sent 15,000 volts of lust through my body. Buy you a coffee?' Not Isa. She half-hid behind the shelf on human physiology and snuck glances at his bleached hair and perfectly straight nose. Smiled when he turned to the side and she saw that he had a streak of blue in his hair. Not a lot – just enough to make him look radical, not off-the-wall. A tasteful streak of blue. And even more devastating: an eyebrow ring. Hell, employment is overrated.

Secondly, most planets' orbits are not perfectly circular. Most are very slightly elliptical. Mars' orbit is significantly elliptical, so the temperature can drop to -133° Celsius in the winter, and increase to a pleasant 30° in summer. Ironweed can survive extreme temperatures, especially cold.

"So, you didn't talk to him?" Doreen barked. As her closest friend, it was her right. Isa would live a quiet life if it weren't for Doreen, Doreen often said.

"No, of course not. What would I say?"

Isa watched Doreen struggle to contain the intensity of her reply with a serious of frustrated gestures and a grunt or two. Doreen was an exclamation point, lacking any sort of sentence or grammatical structure whatsoever. Intentionally unemployed, she'd somehow convinced the welfare system that she was unable to work and gotten onto the long-term recipient list. But there was nothing noticeably wrong with Doreen. She worked out every morning so her limbs were taut and sinewy, her pores clean from daily exertion. She kept her hair cropped short and speckled with red, blond, brown, and black. Doreen was shorter than most women – a mere 5'3", and yet her personality was big enough to make her an Amazon, if amazons would have listened to trip-thrash.

"Just go up, it's a freakin' library! Obviously he's looking at books, just go and strike up a conversation about whatever he's looking at."

"Religious history, thus, anthropology."

"Ah. Damn."

"Let's not assume. He seemed well-groomed. Decent clothes. He has soft eyes."

"Zzzznnn."

"And bleached hair. And an eyebrow ring."

"Oh yeah? Huh."

Third, and most importantly, it draws iron from the soil. Ironweed's life cycle is approximately five years long, and at certain intervals during that time it will release thousands upon thousands of pellet-sized seeds. It grows to a height of seven feet, and its leaves collect the iron until they are solid. This signals the end of its life. The leaves drop off and the plant stalk solidifies, leaving a hollow, tapered pole. Gatherer drones can easily fit one stalk within the next for easy harvest, portage and storage.

Sure, maybe pipes could be made out of it. But this is Usuteshihu. They're not worried about simplifying Earth's plumbing shortages. This plant was designed for Mars. Not only will it extract pure iron from the Martian soil, Ironweed is expected to make the land more fertile and initiate the beginnings of atmosphere, which will eventually trap the heat from the sun, help melt the ice caps, and allow other plants to grow. Sure, Usuteshihu is giving Mars a shot at life, but the byproduct just happens to be scads of building material ready for assembly when the first transports arrive. The trick then will be stopping the plant's production cycle in order to stabilize the atmosphere – but that's something the next three generations of scientists will have to figure out for themselves.

Research Division expects it to take a minimum of 200 years until other plants are able to survive on the surface of Mars. At least 400 before it has an atmosphere that can sustain human life. In the grand scheme of things, 400 years is a speck of sand on an infinite beach. Still, it's a future that Isa will never see. She works for people who will have no idea she even existed. It will likely be 100 years before they can even tell if is the project will succeed. If it does, Usuteshihu will have transformed the future. If not, Isa won't know the difference.

Doreen waited for the perfect nose. She knew Isa would get to that part soon. She always did. This was the way Isa worked: A) find a guy who fit the strict checklist of requirements inside her head, B) daydream about him for a week or two, maybe three, C) realize she will very likely never see him again and D) give up. A perfectly reliable formula, true to her friend's nature. Isa's checklist is as follows:

1) Successful.
2) Educated.
3) Straight nose: a must!
4) Hands: must be just so. There's no way to put it.
5) An open mind: I mean, come on.
6) Hygienic. Beards or tattoos less acceptable. Maybe a T-shirt, but only if it looks like it's recently been ironed, or brand new. Tight pants good: flared OK, boot cut all right, but absolutely not in any way pleated. Pleats were an instant deal breaker.
7) Must not want children.

There were more, although these just came up on a case-by-case basis. For instance, the guy with the Bowler hat. "What would possess someone to wear a hat like that?" Isa asked Doreen, and Doreen, who had secretly owned one of those hats herself for a misguided summer, would simply laugh and get up to order more espresso.

Monday morning. Isa was at the lab before sunrise. After Ironweed, she'd been given a higher salary and an elite team of botanists, geneticists, and geologists. Seven in all.

Cedric Thomas, an aging geneticist, was her number one. He was steadfast, loyal and quiet. Certainly 20 years her elder, she wondered how comfortable he really was with being showed up by a fresh-faced grad after toiling away at Usuteshihu all those years.

Next was Kuma Takeshi, the Japanese botanist. Everyone called him "the Bear." He kind of looked like it, too.

Then Sarah Cohie, the premier authority on Venus. If there was a question as to what conditions were like on Venus, she was the one to ask.

Next in the pecking order was Martina de Silva, the Ecuadorian botanist, whose many years spent in the Amazon studying plants proved invaluable time and again.

Finally, the three geeks: John Speede (Mr. Speed); KGB (Kevin Balfour, nicknamed so because of his initials but also to secretly chill the higher-ups); and Gurjot Manan, who they called The G-Man. They were all computer scientists who worked on DNA coding, and they kind of kept to themselves. They had an unhealthy preoccupation with toy guns – the ones that shoot soft darts. Whenever data was crunching, software was loading, backups were spooling, or someone just got bored, one would sneak attack the others. Weapons were never far out of reach, so open warfare often erupted in the office side.

"Shit!" Doreen said, slamming Isa's door and anchoring herself in the middle of the living room. "They've cut me off! I'm without any income. At all!" Isa stopped petting Nepeta and watched Doreen wait for her reaction. After a few moments, Isa simply shrugged. This pissed Doreen off even more until she reminded herself Isa was a scientist. Isa based her reactions on logic. Of course, Isa's shoulders seemed to say, this was inevitable. Doreen's dropped in response. She agreed. She'd gotten on long-term welfare with no doctors note, no medical proof. In fact, there was no real reason why she couldn't work. Isa was right to be so damned complacent. Well, there was the fact that Doreen could handle very little stress and would often freak out, even when happy. Especially at the slightest change of plans. And this was certainly a change in plans.

Isa expressed her condolence by ordering Doreen a whole-wheat carob biscotti to go with her latte. This was their ritual. Morning coffee at the café in their apartment building. Isa was in a bachelor on the third floor, and Doreen had a two bedroom on the fourth, the 'top floor above Isa' as Doreen often said – one of the few things that secretly irritated Isa whenever Doreen mentioned it. On the main floor was Café Literal, the Iseetan vacuum repair shop, and a real estate agent. The building was all hardwood so no one purchased vacuums and it wasn't the sort of building that people live in just before they buy houses, so the other two businesses certainly didn't survive from the Oxford Arms' patronage. But the café? They did well. "So what are you going to do?"

"I have no flipping clue," said Doreen, exasperated. Welfare had come so easily for her, just like the cheques from her corporate dad had done before. Isa often wondered what Doreen told them at the government office when she applied for assistance. She had imagined the welfare people would do background checks and require thorough documentation, thus finding out that Doreen was penniless on the street because of a philosophical difference. That she had grown up in utter splendor. She was amazed at Doreen's ability to get on the recipient list in the first place, then to get her payments upped to slightly above minimum wage. By social welfare standards, that was luxury living. Perhaps it had been easier to give her what she wanted to get her out of their offices, or an official oversight. Either way, they had practically thrown money at her for three years now. Isa never figured out how, but her accountant knew it had made tax season more painful for her than it should have been.

"Christ, Isa – I'm going to have to work! What the hell can I do? I'm not qualified for anything."

Isa considered arguing but Doreen was right. Psychology degree. Almost as bad as anthropology. Different discipline, same trick.

"I will check the postings at work. I suspect we employ psychologists, though it's just speculation, but if not I'm sure there is office help required."

"What? That's a dead end job. Working for the government? You get sucked in by the paycheck, and next thing you know, you're middle-aged , fat, complacent, with no hope of ever getting out." Doreen plunged a spoon into her latte and indulged in a whole pack of sugar to blur the despair.

"You do recall that I work there."

"Yeah, but you're an expert. You're actually using your degree. Office work? I might as well work at the post office. Have you seen those uniforms? I wouldn't survive.

"Actually, you may be right."

The problems with Venus are multifold. You might think for a planet with a similar size, mass, and density to Earth, there would be few. But for instance, it's hot. Extremely hot. The temperature on Venus exceeds 400° Celsius at any given time, due to an atmosphere made of 96% carbon dioxide. That puts Earth's global warming to shame. That kind of heat changes plants into dust instantly, so Cedric's job was to find a way to alter and intensify the genetic code in the hardiest desert plants. His section of the lab was filled with cacti. He'd take cuttings, blend them up, extract the long DNA chains, and study them at great length. He would then work with Kuma the Bear to seek out what made them so resistant to the heat, and they would take their findings to Isa. Her task was to figure out how to instruct the plant to create a thick enough exterior to keep its moisture from boiling away under such extreme conditions. She would come up with lists of possible solutions and have the geeks work on calculating the coding on these needle-in-a-haystack searches, while Martina speculated on ways to extend plants' light response cycles. Venus' solar revolution is opposite that of Earth, so its day lasts longer than its year – less impressive than it sounds because one Venusian day is just 243 Earth days long. But because of this, the plant would have to survive darkness for 243 days straight, while surviving a day of approximate equal length. Tall enough order, but when you throw into the mix no water vapor and clouds of sulfuric acid, it seems impossible to create anything that will survive.

But Isa doesn't believe in the impossible. Not at work, anyway. Not on a cellular level.

The answer came in a glass. She was sitting on a patio waiting for Doreen when the waitress set down her lemonade and walked away. Suddenly, the answer. A possible solution anyway, and a simple one. Isa was embarrassed not to have seen it sooner.

A plant adapts to benefit from its environment, even in the face of dramatic changes in short periods of time. Look at the crickets, who evolved a noiseless variant in just a few short years. Look at humans, who boosted their problem-solving abilities, increased hand-eye coordination, and found greater levels of patience with the development of video games. The solution was everywhere – in the air around her, in the concrete at her feet. In her glass. Simply take the acidic atmosphere and make it work for you. Earth had many plants with a taste for acid. Isa would grow some kind of lemon on Venus.

When Doreen arrived they talked for a full 35 minutes before Isa mentioned she may have solved the Venus problem. Doreen sat dumfounded, amazed and openly aghast that Isa could continue on with her day as normal – so calm mere minutes after potentially solving the kind of problem that took lesser scientists a lifetime. How was it possible? What was going on in her brain? How come she wasn't freaking out? Isa shrugged, downed her lemonade and remembered she had to stop for cat food on their way home. Doreen wondered how normal her best friend really was.

The Oxford Arms was close enough to downtown to walk, yet still on a relatively quiet street. Two blocks from the subway station, two blocks from a grocery store, and all within four square blocks of 12 coffee shops and six pubs with patios. Important for a thriving, sun-beaten overpopulation. The Oxford Arms was also five blocks from the main branch of the public library. Doreen had sworn off the place after the last two guys she checked out both had extremely short due dates and higher than average return fees. She wondered why Isa had started noticing the men there only after Doreen had regaled her with two long tales of woe. But eventually she realized that Isa lived in her lab for days on end and when she could squeeze a late night outing into her busy agenda, it was usually spent with

Doreen – the two of them so caught up in catching up that they ignored everyone else. Besides, the best male specimens were asleep at that time of morning anyway.

The rent at the Oxford was cheap, and they allowed cats. Isa moved in just as she'd started graduate studies, and stayed simply because it was easier than looking for something else, and human genes are designed to find the easiest route through most things. It was a distinguished little building, with only a few disadvantages. For one, it was a fire trap, should a fire ever occur. But chances of that were acceptably small since they had upgraded to electric stoves. Also, every floor in the building creaked like toads, so you could hear the newlyweds upstairs each time they would entwine and stumble blindly from whatever room to the bedroom. You could also hear the chubby guy with the cane as he hobbled down the hallway each day at seven and again at four. And, of course, it was radiator heat. That meant that it was never perfectly warm. It was always too hot by the radiator and too cold at Isa's desk. Luckily, Nepeta was a lap cat, always ready to curl up and keep Isa warm. Cats are good that way. Something to cuddle, to hold.

But the guy. She'd almost forgotten him in her hyper-focused state this past month, and now there he was in the coffee shop, ordering a coffee from Jane the teen barista – right in the building. Her building! Had he moved into the area? Had he moved into her building? She had to get to the lab before Cedric, so she couldn't wait around to see which exit the guy took. She'd asked Jane later but the girl had only remembered the flurry of orders that morning. Not even the blue streak could spark recollection. Isa took this to mean he was only passing through by chance. Interesting. At third sighting he was too far away to catch in time. At fourth, Isa decided to do the unthinkable – to be late for an important meeting with Doreen to find out where he was going. It was a chilly day, and overcast. One token rainy day to remind people what that had felt like back before the dry hot dust had taken over. He was wrangling an umbrella that had blown wrong-side-out in the wind. His straight hair was combed down to the side and hung squarely over one eye, and he wore a black wool coat and jeans. She couldn't tell what kind.

It was Thursday evening. Sevenish, maybe. Isa had been on her way to Doreen's gym when she spotted him and was forced still by a sudden decision. Best friend? Or painfully cute guy?

Isa stood and watched him drift away, still paralyzed with indecision. The plan was to help Doreen refine her self-sales pitch before she met with the owner at 7:30. Doreen would already be at the gym, desperately needing moral support. But there he went, drifting away from her again. It was nearly a month since the last sighting. This was usually when they disappeared.

Tough decision. Isa checked her watch. She might be able to do both. Maybe. If not, Doreen would agree with her decision. She told herself that again. Then once more as she derailed and lurched off after him, hoping Doreen would somehow understand and not lose her temper right there at the check-in desk.

Doreen came to the gym every day of the week, but today was radically different. Doreen was applying for a job there. What could be a better fit? Ok, it wasn't, really. It seemed awful to her, actually. A sullying of her sacred haven. Doreen feared that as soon as she worked there, she'd no longer want to come in, and really, what else did she do? It was that and the café. And, well, there was also the skateboard shop, and the place she went to pick up guys. She sometimes thought she was getting too old for the guys who frequented the place, but the guys that were her age were known as 'lifers.' That was all they were ever going to do, and scarce few of them would get to be a legend. Where the hell was Isa? She had never been late. Not even once. A wave of worry washed over her and sank to the base of her neck, where it joined a single bead of worried perspiration.

The guy, even at a leisurely rainy-day pace, weaved through the downtown crowds easily and had a big lead on her. Isa would scramble across shortcuts and charge through puddles to make up time. She'd think she was gaining, but he was like an eel, easily working the currents, sidestepping impossibly cumbersome strollers and sandwich board signs, ducking open umbrellas and skipping through busy traffic like a gazelle sailing over the underbrush in long, effortless strides.

Isa was not an eel. She felt like a mule. Thinking she would stay and catch up on a few hundred missed dates with the elliptical machine while she waited for Doreen, she had dressed for the gym. Truly unsightly sweat pants hung loosely from her. Highly practical for splashing down sidewalks at high speeds, but also the least attractive piece of clothing known to humankind. What was she thinking? She must note this incident and from today onwards, always be prepared for just such an encounter. Next time she would plan better and change at the gym.

The sweat pant factor meant that actually talking to him today was out of the question. Perhaps she had made the wrong choice in her pursuit? But, no – he hadn't been back to the library and the sightings were dwindling off, so discovering his coordinates was the priority for the day. She clumsily tried to keep up with him, but there was something about the sleekness of movement, his agility. Isa was tall, but usually nimble. Today it seemed she had bumped into everything on the street. Was it nerves?

She followed him for five blocks before he lost her at the corner. She was hoping he'd stop somewhere, maybe at some regular spot he frequented on regular days. A place where he sat alone, because in her fantasy world he was single. No luck in the corner café. She thought he was gone altogether until she spotted his coattail disappearing into a multi-story brownstone. Was this where he lived? The building had six flats. A quick scan of the buzzers and she had his last name committed to memory before she skated off to avoid detection.

Well, she knew six last names, and one of them was potentially his, as long as the landlord had kept the buzzers up to date and there was no female counterpart whom he was visiting, or worse, who had preceded his residency.

Six surnames could be worked into so many permutations.

"So, is this romance, or are you a stalker?" Doreen asked. Again, at Café Literal, the same Thursday just before the eleven o'clock closing time. The workout had gone well. Fuelled by adrenaline, Isa had taken on her mortal enemy, the Stairmaster, and survived.

"I'm not a stalker!" Isa said, swirling another hypnotic spiral of sugar into her decaf latte.

"If he's interested, and available – which you still haven't found out I remind you – it's cute. Maybe even romantic. But if he's got a girlfriend, or a wife and kids? That makes you a prime candidate for a restraining order. What's next? Breaking into his apartment and sleeping in his bed?"

"I had to find out."

"Oh don't be so damn serious. Let's see the list."

There were six names on it.

B. Harden
D. James
B. Ross
C. Penny
J. Corria
M. Richardson

"So one of these people is your mystery man."

"Potentially."

"Yeah ok, potentially. So how does this information help solve the mystery of your mystery man?"

"Well, Say his name is Bob Harden. Bobby? That sounds nice. You can tell a lot by a person's name."

"You're psychotic."

"Or Daniel James. Who would that person be? They type to make seductive eye contact with a stranger when involved with someone in a serious capacity?"

'God. I'm going to bed."

The owner had taken Doreen's resume but left the quasi-interview to a new girl who worked the front desk. She was a certain species of bubbly blond that seems to thrive in the gym ecosystem. Their surface enticing, but beneath, the perfume of a darker agenda. Doreen was neither bubbly nor blond, but she could have easily bench pressed this girl, so maybe there was a shot.

"Christopher Penny. John Corria. No, I don't like that one. If that's him, I may have to reconsider."

"Goodnight psycho. Happy psychosis night. If you can't sleep, don't call me to read out more names. I've heard enough."

The theory is that using an ironweed graft, you can encourage the skin of a lemon to have sufficient tensile properties that will allow it to resist dehydration. The problem is that the lemon grows on a tree. Growing trees in a 400° desert is no easy feat. So that left Cedric and Martina the unfathomable task of trying to grow lemon on a succulent plant, namely a cactus. Plus, you're trying to develop a lemon that utilizes sulfuric acid in place of water, with a peel that can withstand the extreme levels of heat and sunlight bestowed upon Venus. Plus, an atmospheric pressure equivalent to the pressure found one mile under earth's oceans. So far, after 193 genetic trials, they were still at square one. They could produce genetic chains and create a type of seed, but the seed was non-productive. Even if they survived the Venusian simulation chamber – a vat of boiling acid which Martina called the cauldron – but the seeds would remain dormant. No spark. No chispa. Eventually it would succumb to the pressure, and that was it. Lost. So far the environment was proving far too harsh for anything to survive.

To say that Gail had a strong personality was an understatement. Much shorter than Isa but with the same mouse-brown hair, Isa's mother Gail had corrected her overbite years ago. She averted crow's feet and maintained a perfect complexion with diet, exercise, immense water consumption, and a series of products based on the sacred watermelon plant. Like Isa, she was obsessed with the practical and commercial uses of plant matter. Especially those with magical restorative properties. Especially those that smelled irresistible. She was passionate about her products and about utilizing nature as it was intended, so Gail had never forgiven her child for refusing to go into business with her but choosing instead a life of genetic manipulations. She had never forgiven Isa for a lot of things.

The commercial venture was Fresh Face, an organic skin care store, and all products were cruelty free, all smelling like limes or peaches or some other fruit. Gail had turned make-up and soap into a multi-sensual experience. And on her company's funds, she'd fly around the world looking for the newest make-up process, the latest soap based in the oldest homeopathic formulas. Gail had never married and seeing her friend's after 20 years of matrimony, never looked back on this as a bad decision.

Calls to her mom were to be made on Sunday nights, when the rates were cheaper. At least it must be Sunday night wherever in the world Gail was. Could be Frankfurt, Tokyo, Sao Paulo – anywhere there were a chain of Fresh Face stores. Isa never bothered to point out that rates were not cheaper at the times she would be calling.

"It's so cold here in Frankfurt. Tragic for the skin, which means we should do very well here. And pollution! It's worse than Mexico City."

"Actually, Mom, I think Mexico City wins that one. According to studies."

"According to studies. I've been there. Have you? Mexico City is a filthy place, but the air at the resorts is clean, and the food is just wonderful. You should see all the cars here in Germany. They're smaller, but they drive so fast and European style, so you never know where they are coming from. It's simply impossible to navigate without the GPS."

Even after Isa hung up, her mother's chatter would haunt her through the day. Sometimes it even sent her into the lab to focus her energy on something – anything – productive and drown out that nattering, critical dialogue.

On Monday booked the day off sick. That was unusual, but he was nearing retirement, so no one faulted him. They didn't know this was the first sick day he had ever taken at Usuteshihu. They didn't know he had artfully dodged his wife for 20 years and now was in bed being nurtured by this nit-picking drone that was bursting with regrets and complaints.

Feeling a little lost with Cedric's absence, the geeks worked away on their computers and the morning was spent without a single air attack. However, The G-Man had picked up a new air-propulsion weapon on the weekend and eventually could resist no longer. Within seconds ten padded darts were whizzing towards monitors and heads, bouncing off multiple surfaces and causing far too much noise for Usuteshihu's overzealous security guards. But they were bought off easily enough with junk from the off-limits Geek fridge. KGB had been leading the arms race up to that point, equipped with an engine he'd devised himself, capable of firing three simultaneous darts. His method allowed for multiple surprise-based hits, but made for longer reloads during crucial counter attacks. Each man paid a minor fortune for extra ammo, but other than home electronics, they spent their money frugally, being under twenty-five and never having seen the inside of a bar nor an airplane.

And there he was! At a coffee shop somewhere between her place and his. Maybe he stopped on the way home from work, Isa hoped. He had his laptop out. A good sign. There were sufficient resources for a laptop. Maybe he was a professor at the university. How could she talk to him? Why was she being forced to make the first move? Coffee shops were so difficult. The was no turning back once you'd ordered. And so many choices! Opening sentences were quintessential. Over his shoulder, she could see that he was typing something out. That would do. Gripping the largest possible latte, Isa waited expectantly until the patrons at the next tiny table gave her a long look, decided she wouldn't leave their side, and vacated.

She sat. Sipped. Coughed a little. Readied herself to speak, finally, and found herself remarkably unprepared.

"Work?" she asked, nonchalantly. Then felt her face flinch in embarrassment. He looked up. She hadn't noticed he was plugged in, listening to music.

"Did you say something?" He tugged out one ear bud, but still had the other in. Bad sign.

"Uh... working? On something?" she gulped, pointing at the computer.

"Oh. Just, you know, writing stuff."

This wasn't working out as planned. A good first move on her part would have radically changed the script. But in fact she was dangerously close to botching this up completely.

Asking the correct question could have transitioned naturally into conversation, like, 'yes this is a proposal for an Brazilian airline I'm starting.' Or, 'In fact I am on deadline – my votes for this year's Nobel Prize laureates must be submitted by noon tomorrow.' But no, thanks to her asinine mumbling, he was simply writing 'stuff.' What was wrong with her faculties? And what kind of man didn't say hello? Why had she ordered such a massive coffee in a stay-in mug? Now she was stuck here, suffering this state of long-awaited perdition. And he was staring at her and it was up to her to speak again and she could almost hear the digital numbers shift the lines on her watch from one second to the next, crawling ever forward until it would mark a full minute of silence. She must speak now.

"Oh, are you a writer?" she asked. He pulled out the second earplug of his headset. Thank God. He smiled at her. His nose was nice and straight, even this close. She concentrated on the blushing warmth of the coffee cup.

"No. Nothing that official. It's for my blog. Really, I'm just killing time. I like to get the spelling right, so I put it in MS Word first, because I like the spell check."

God. A blog. And an overly detailed description of menial processes. What could those two factors mean? It was now or never. Isa crossed her legs and extended a hand. "Isa. I'm Isa. Isabella, but I go by Isa." She was trying to shift into a pleasing, sultry voice.

"David." He took her hand and shook it and it was warm and enveloping. The grip was firm but not overly tight, confident but inviting. His hand felt just so. Perfectly just so.

Isa quickly scanned her memory. D. James. That must be him. He was the only D on the list. David James. She was happy he said David, and not Dave. A Dave is nice, but a David? A David is hot. He was hot. And suddenly she was overheating, with the coffee and the handshake. She took off her jacket.

"I've seen you around," he said. "You came in here before, about a week ago, right?"

"Yes!" she said, a little too excitedly. She slouched a little and pressed her lips tight before turning them into a smile. He'd noticed her. Then she realized that he had seen her two weeks ago, on the rainy day, on the day she'd tracked him down to his apartment building. Had he known she was following him the whole time? She tried to breathe.

Then, the dreaded infinite uncomfortable pause. They sat relatively motionless both trapped in that terrible space between what you want to say and what you can't say, that leaves only boring safe things in the middle of a panicked scramble that is the need to offer up interesting small talk.

"Blog? What's it about?"

"Yeah. It's… it's kind of stupid. It's a Star Wars thing."

Could there be a worse sign? No. Not even if he had been wearing a ring. Star Wars? A Star Wars blog?! "It's a Star Wars blog" is one of the last sentences a girl wants to hear from a guy she is interested in getting to know better. Star Wars blog leads her mind instantly to the following conclusions: A) this is an emotionally stunted guy who thinks about little other than science fiction. B) The upside of that is that he's probably not in a relationship. C) The downside of that is that I will likely not wish to remain in a relationship with an emotionally stunted guy. D) Emotionally stunted guys are sometimes overly eager to please potential mates, which can be either D) i. An extremely good thing, or D) ii. Terrible.

Actually, she'd secretly dated a comic guy once in high school. He'd bat around names of superheroes and secret identities with his friends, but sometimes when they were alone he pointed that cannon at Isa. Kyle Rainer, he'd say, and then wait a moment to see if he had to explain it. The new Green Lantern? Alan Scott was the original, but now he was Sentinel, and Hal Jordan was the second Green Lantern, but he went mad and killed all of the Green Lantern Corps before dying and becoming the new Spectre. And that's when Kyle Rainer took over, but that's not even mentioning Guy Gardener or Kilowog or the rest of them. Isa did nothing. Smile. Wait in hope that he could be once again convinced to share his extensive knowledge of kissing techniques instead.

"Oh, yeah Star Wars. The last one was good, wasn't it?"

"Not as good as the originals. Without Luke, Han, and Leah, the chemistry isn't there."

Isa had waited months to talk to this man. This exotic stranger with the eyebrow ring and the tuft of not-too-rebellious blue. And as she sat there listening to a five-minute diatribe on the inferiority of the new Star Wars movies – What the hell was that Jar Jar guy? A fish and horse mixed together? And not even a nice fish. One of those bony bottom feeders, with vaguely racist underpinnings – she felt her coffee chill to frigid.

"Was it worth nine hours of waiting while you watched the politics of the Jedi Knights?"

"Are you still talking to me?

"Oh my God. Sorry. I get kind of caught up – That's what I do. I'm part of an Internet Jedi Council. I do this for 10 hours a day."

As the words left his beautiful, slightly lopsided mouth, Isa felt like she was had just been immersed in the cauldron herself.

In the last six months on the Venus project, the cactus plan had been forced to change. Faced with successive failures, they would strive for more of a vine, something that could support the weight of the ironclad lemons. Venusian gravity is similar to that of Earth. The structure of the plant didn't have to be that stable – not as it would be if they were engineering a plant for Saturn or Jupiter. Mars had less gravity, but it had been a nightmare to calculate all possible ramifications of the motion of those weighty iron leaves. Venus? There gravity was a simple computation in an extremely difficult project. They tried to imbue the vine with a steely bark that encased a softer interior.

The lemons would thrive on the plant's acidic liquid supply. Kuma came up with the theory. He was thinking about honeysuckles, and so he started looking into *Lonicera japonica*, and the genetic structure looked adequate. It would need to be much, much bigger, and but for now The Venusian Lemon Vine had no restrictions on size. There were, however, several thousand other restrictions be accounted for. After two years of failure, the team was nearing completion of the first seed from the new batch. It was looking good.

Tethered rather tenuously to the ground herself, Doreen needed work and fast. Welfare and the secret savings donated by her mom when she first left home had dried up. There was never going to be a call from the gym, not even with an ocean of blonde hair dye. Doreen's muscles didn't overcome her lack of social skills, and she knew it. And her last cheque was being cashed today. Rent, food, her gym membership. She had one month before she was back out on the street. She had elected to keep the membership even though it wasn't cheap, and they'd been disloyal to her. She paid it not because she had signed one of those eighteen-month deals that they are always pushing on people, and it hadn't expired. She paid it because this gym had always been her refuge no matter what was going on, and she couldn't refuse it its due. So, this was her last cheque. That meant Doreen needed a resume. A CV, she'd call it, to sound more European. That meant a little time in Isa's apartment, with Isa's computer. Isa never used it anyway.

Despite the flash submersion in her emotional acid-bath, Isa had exchanged numbers with David. A very good sign! Great for Isa, who usually she didn't get this far. In fact, she didn't usually make it to the talking stage, so having a pocket full of digits was nearing miraculous. She had, of course, memorized it instantly, but checked it against the original often and repeated it to herself whenever she needed a moment of distraction. Many of her moments proved to have this need, right up until the fourth day. The day her telephone rang.

"Hello?" Doreen said. The resume wasn't going so well. With no actual work since university, that being seven years ago, it was hard to bulk up her experience section.

"Hi, uh, Isa?"

"As if," Doreen said. "Who's this? Are you selling something? What would you like me to buy, sexy-voiced stranger?"

"Do I have… Does Isa live at this number?"

"Yeah,. She does. Hey are you that guy? She's here. Do you wanna speak to her?"

After two minutes of silent freaking out, pacing, and preparatory throat-clearing, Isa was on the phone with David James. She pictured his eyebrow ring as he spoke. His voice was so soft and lilting as they took turns fumbling through the first few conversations. Then, a minor miracle.

"So Isa. I've got a free evening tomorrow. Any chance you'd come to an art show with me? There's something going on at the NEU gallery. I don't remember exactly what it's about, but my sister gave me an invitation. It says there will be food."

"Yeah. Sure. That sounds excellent."

Excellent? Was she back at the lab, adjudicating a new specimen? Maybe he could direct her to an Internet counsel for people who are talented in science but have minimal skill at social interaction.

A person can tell what their new hairstyle is going to look like before it happens by the look of the stylist. If your stylist has big hair, you know they're going to think big when it comes to your hair. If your stylist looks like someone's mom, prepare for a mom cut. Martina's friend was not going to give Isa anything matronly. She was a fusion of big hair, badass accessories, and kid chic. Isa had talked her into a geometric bob, hair sprayed up for the evening, but still something she could pin back at the lab. Eschewing the complimentary make-up 'touch up', Isa made a quick excuse to go home, and put on some things Martina had made her buy. A pale light base powder. Dark burgundy lipstick to make her lips look bigger. Blue liner to compliment her auburn eyes. The stylist had wanted to highlight and lowlight Isa's hair, but there wasn't time. It'd be nice to get away from the mouse-brown, especially when David had bleached and blue hair. But he'd have to settle for au naturale.

"Men want to be fathers, you know? They want to be a Dad. It's hardwired into them."

"Some of them. You're presuming." Doreen said, watching Isa's third attempt at outlining her eye lid.

"Most of them! They all think of stupid things like running behind a bicycle, or throwing baseballs. They think of hockey and swimming lessons, and Disneyland, and having a little buddy to share root beer with. How can I compete with a normal, curvaceous, high-estrogen female? I can't! It's hardwired into the human physiology. Reproduce. Reproduce!"

Doreen just shrugged. "As if."

Martina didn't shrug. She hugged. "Do you actually think he won't love you because of the children? So what? Many, many couples don't have children. I never wanted to, and that doesn't stop the men from being interested in me." Martina had a mane of bottle-red hair, and even though deep into her forties, the geeks were all secretly in love with her. There was something about her Ecuadorian uniqueness that drew people to her.

"There's more to it than that. You know there's more."

"He won't care. You're so beautiful, with that cute little smile, and those eyes. Oh, he'll be melting. And you keep yourself in shape, yes? The men like that!"

"I don't understand men. I never did. Not for one second."

"Look, you get yourself dressed up tonight. Put some make-up on. Make yourself pretty. You want him to like you, yes? Before you say goodnight, wipe off the lipstick, because there'll be enough left over that he won't notice, and when he kisses you he doesn't just get the taste of lipstick. He gets the taste of your spell."

"Martina!"

"And not too much hairspray. Just a little. You want it to look touchable. Men like that."

The newspaper is no place to find a job. It's another joke. It's the carrot in front of the donkey cart. There are really two job advertisements in the job section of the newspaper. That job is already taken. The boss' cousin has the job, or his friend, or the cute guy from the other floor. There is no job vacancy, but there's bureaucracy, and thus, they need to 'advertise' a job that isn't available, for political reasons. So they put an ad in the paper, take in applications, and give the job to their cousin, or the cute guy, according to plan. The second job is the one where you work but don't make any money. They're the ones that promise high returns on minimal investment, which actually translates as you end up with nothing but the product you had to invest in. The knife set you must display to customers, or the vacuum, or whatever vitamin supplement the pyramid scheme is selling. Only bottom-of-the-barrel jobs appear in the paper. Although after walking around the shopping mall and dropping her resume off at the sports stores and the bakery, there wasn't much else to do. The paper thoroughly searched, and nothing found, Doreen went to the gym for what felt like it would be her last super-sets.

When taking a date to the art gallery, it's a good idea to know something about art. A couple current names, or something about popular works from art history to compare the new stuff against. Isa didn't know a single thing. It turned out for the best, though, because David didn't either. They both walked around the gallery, admiring the work without spending too much time trying to comprehend it, mainly because they wanted to the other to think they already comprehend it.

"Sometimes it isn't about understanding, just appreciating. He really uses a lot of paint."

"You're right, David. That sure is a lot of paint." Probably two inches thick, with layers of browns and greens, the artist had sliced into the surface to demonstrate depth.

"I kind of like it. I like the greens."

"Me too."

At least the Oxford Arms was cat friendly, Isa thought, closing the door to her apartment.

Six apartments in the four-story building housed five cats and one of those shaky little Mexican dogs on the third floor next to Isa. Dogs weren't allowed, but Streus, the owner, had made a simple but concise argument to keep Hefe, saying Mexican dogs aren't really dogs, because just look at it. That, combined with Streus' weight problem and bad leg was enough for the landlord to give him the go ahead. Walking a big dog would have been too stressful on the poor guy, and an indoor cat wouldn't have given him any exercise at all. It was a good compromise.

The overzealous couple upstairs had a cat. Tom. Nepeta's arch enemy. They'd been in the hallway at the same time twice now, and fur had flown. Both times Doreen had intervened, because she was upstairs right across from the couple and above Streus and Hefe.

Neko, the Japanese girl on the second floor had two cats, both with names seemingly unpronounceable to Isa's Anglo tongue.

Jimmy, aka Seven, had also gotten a cat since moving in. Jimmy played brilliant Brazilian jazz, samba, and chorinho, no doubt because he had seven fingers on each hand. Isa often tried to convince him that he wasn't the least bit freakish: his physiology had merely adapted to handle the intricate maneuvers and complex fingerings his family's playing style required. His father had seven fingers on each hand as well, as did his grandfather and his two uncles. His cousin was born without the extra digits, and his other uncle was still young, and hadn't had any children yet. It may be possible that Seven was the last of the line. Isa doubted it. For his calling, he was better adapted than most to difficult chording, plucking, and technical finesse. He played for 6 or more hours a day. Yet he rarely petted his cat. Isa suspected that his cat was there merely to entice his neighbor Neko to come over and visit, but Isa suspected the plan would fail within the month and the cat would migrate to Neko's on its own.

Isa was disappointed there had been no kiss, but nothing happens in one day, she reasoned. Especially when dealing with the genetic structure of a lemon tree, trying to turn it into a cactus-like vine, send it to Venus, and ensure it thrive. Still, they were on the verge of the new experiment. She could feel it. It wouldn't be long. They were doing a test today at 2:00. Would it survive? Would the seed be incinerated before it could sprout? Isa was thinking about David, and the date. There were so many things that could go wrong. She ate lunch with Martina. Martina understood her. Their world was filled with life, with plants of every kind and, and many animals, but scarce few people. It was foreign ground, especially to Isa. Though better adapted to social norms, Martina had also spent years in the Amazon jungle, studying plants and going off for days on end, only coming back to camp to refill her canteen. She drank from the water vine, sure, but after a few days of water vine, you need a tall glass of something purified and cold.

Cedric wished to adjust his television's volume. As days passed, his wife and neighbors all came to believe he was rapidly going deaf, and he believed that if he couldn't get his wife to stop talking and leave the house, he would go deaf in self-defense.

Maybe the art gallery wasn't the best idea, but there was little pressure, too, because they could look at something and discuss it, getting to know one another's tastes a little before the inevitable coffee afterwards. He suggested Café Literal, in the Oxford Arms. She didn't let him know that she lived in the building, not yet. Not until after. She'd find a way to make a joke out of walking her home by taking him around the block or something. Isa liked him, and that meant she was terrified. Her hypothesis about the anthropology degree proved true, which was naturally, both good and bad. Bad because he was not currently employed, but somehow used his knowledge to make money by tracking the interwoven cultures of the life forms found in the Star Wars universe. He also sold interesting collectables he found in junk shops online. His degree was good because it made him yearn to travel, and what's more appealing that the allure of travel? Successful creation of a new plant species, she supposed, but other than that, not much.

Isa didn't tell him what she did for a living. She said she worked with plants in a lab. That was enough for now.

The genetic structure of plants is actually quite similar, even across species. With a glance you can tell right if it's plant or an animal code under the glass. You can look deeper and figure out what a plant will look like and how it will behave. With people, the simplest gesture is impossible to comprehend. Even animal structures have more variance between them than plant structures. It's interesting, because life on Earth originated from a tiny one-celled plant, which somehow, mysteriously, came to be into existence.

Isa didn't dismiss the possibility that life came to Earth on an asteroid. It wouldn't take much. One cell, finding a planet that just happened to have the right atmosphere, gravity, and of course, the moon, pulling at the oceans and creating tides to keep everything stirred up.

Another theory claimed life was implanted here. Life specifically designed to evolve and adapt to the atmospheric conditions of Earth, possibly even designed to create humans after a billion years of evolution. Perhaps by a team of scientists like Isa's.

Or, there were arguments for the spontaneous, self-generated creation of life. How did it happen? How is life created from nothing? That's where some people reach out for God, or for Chaos Theory, or whatever means of defining their beliefs are handy and acceptable at the time. Isa weighed the different possibilities often, but still reserved judgment. It did, however, make for an interesting conversation over coffee.

Almost as interesting as the goodnight gesture David had made.

"He had a tattoo, but a forgivable one. A Welsh dragon. His grandfather was a sailor in world war two and had the same tattoo, so I understood its significance."

"Mmmm. So did he kiss you or what? Did he come upstairs?"

"Huh!" Isa twirled her spoon distractedly for what far too long.

Doreen loved her friend, and she adored the surge of voyeuristic romance, but she hated her own life too, and that was starting to overshadow the joy. Still, she begged for details. How was the art? What did you talk about on the walk to Café Literal? How was the goodbye. A kiss? No? A hug? Yes, but a good hug. A long one. And talk of a later meeting, maybe on the weekend. A truly excellent sign.

Martina and the geeks took Cedric flowers, which they did not regret until he forced them to tell him every detail of the project a fourth time, gripping Martina's hands until they were slightly numb and grey-blue.

The new seed was all but done. In two weeks it would be inserted in the Atmospheric Simulator. Two weeks, and then another possibility for success, or another defeat to add to the calculations. They'd been here before, 117 times in 28 months. They figured they might have finally managed to acidic problem this time. Although she had broking virgin ground on Ironweed, it had been easier. Repeating the miracle was starting to be frustrating. Maybe there just wasn't a way for there to be life on Venus. Maybe it was time to give up. Two weeks until they did it again. Isa prayed there would be no more miscarriages. One hundred and seventeen times the team turned back to their desks or dishes or microscopes and set their minds on trying again. But it was starting to get them down.

In many ways the second date was better than the first. There was less of that nervous tension, less fear of the unknown. They'd been there once, on a date, together, so there was still the anticipation of the first kiss and of what followed. Now they could start being themselves.

He'd suggested a movie, but Isa didn't think that was a good date. No conversation, dark room, and what if he was a movie talker? She couldn't abide that during the one and only movie she would have seen in seven years. Instead they agreed to dinner, on Saturday. That carried a little bit of pressure. A Saturday dinner meant that he was giving up his Saturday to spend it with her. It was a minor commitment, but a commitment nonetheless.

Doreen had gotten a call from a job. Just an interview, but it was something. Better than the nothingness of the gym. Sporting goods, covering free weights and fitness wear. She had no interpersonal skills to speak of, but she was muscular, and that would appeal. Maybe she could work out a way to sell active wear using psychological insecurities. She shuddered at the depths of her own desperation.

"One thing I don't want you to know about me?" David said, responding to the question with an upbeat air that suggested no hidden daemons. "Man, that's a tough one. So far I've told you several things that would chase away most girls. Membership on the Jedi Council."

"Greetings, Jedi James. You are now logged in."

"Yeah yeah, go ahead and bash me, I can take it. But I'm working on a few papers in my spare time, I'll be society-approved soon enough."

"And?"

"Oh yeah. Something that I don't want you to know. Oh – I saw a flying saucer once."

"Oh. Really?" Isa stiffened.

"Yeah. I was young, like, nine maybe? You know, the age when everything seems unreal anyway, when you look back. So I might've made it up."

"Of course you did."

"No, really, I know that physics is against me here, but I was out at my uncle's farm. It was night, and I was suppose to watch for coyotes and yell if they came around. They laid low during the day, but at night they came after the chickens. So I was cutting through the field on the far side of the coop, when suddenly there was a brilliant white light all around me. It came from nowhere. It was like there an enormous helicopter had just above me, except it had lights all around it, in a circle, all shining into my face, but I could still see into it without it hurting my eyes. Then it was gone."

"Space invaders. No wonder you became a sci-fi geek."

"Now tell me yours."

"Absolutely not."

"Come on! I've done nothing but confess embarrassing stuff to you. That's heaps of ammunition for you to reject me with, and you've given me nothing."

Silence.

"You're a scientist. You have no siblings. What else? Hit me with something really good. Something I can retaliate with for years."

That overzealous offering silenced them both for a bit.

Isa had her secret, but she wasn't ready to tell it yet. So once again, she softened the truth. She explained that she was one of those dreaded cat owners who treated the cat like a child. She talked to her, cooked her special meals like salmon with wheat grass, and cradled her rather obsessively until the cat found an escape route.

The cat was her baby replacement.

Either: A) He hadn't picked up on the significant tone in her voice. B) He didn't want to know because it would signal the end for them. C) Kids didn't matter to him. D) He was thinking about something completely unrelated. E) He was thinking about sex. It drove Isa mad that she could not easily formulate which response was true.

Monday was turning out to be difficult. The code for the lemon vine was ready. They knew it, but they needed approval from Usuteshihu to begin creating the seeds, and that meant presenting the existing test results. Not only was this the thesis defense, they'd been struggling for so long, fighting the lethargy of failure after failure. If they did it right, they would get the green light. But Cedric was generally the voice of their team. How could they do it without him? Usuteshihu had protocols. Specific restrictions. Legal issues. Rules about how things worked. So Monday was spent checking and rechecking, the geeks not able to fire a single shot as they went over and over the CG model of the lemon vine weathering the volatile environmental conditions. Everyone took one more look. They all yearned to surge ahead, but they couldn't get anyone to open the gate. Being the most passionate, Martina was the least able to contain her resentment at not just jumping into the fun part of the project. Everyone felt that way, except those who funded the experiment. On something like this, Usuteshihu was god.

At home, Cedric was face to face with his own God. He lay on the kitchen floor, the taste of sour wine and anti-platelet medication on his tongue. He'd been feeling so much better he had a glass of port before supper, and thought it tasted sour and terrible. His wife thought it was fine but he thought she was simply being contradictory. Then he felt a burst of indigestion and his arm hurt. He knew what was happening. He told his wife just seconds before it hit. They had expected it, but didn't believe it was possible. As the ambulance came screaming up the street, Cedric closed his eyes. The sirens wailed. His wife howled even louder for him to get up off the floor.

There was something about Cedric. He was in his late fifties, early sixties, and was brilliant, no question. He could easily have been project manager for an easier task, but that wasn't his style. He had kept most of his hair, although it was pure white. There was the aura of respect about him. Was it his age that did that? Everyone deferred to his suggestions, recognizing their merit, and he always listened intently to Isa. He understood her brilliance and was not threatened by it, which was also part of his charm. There was no time wasted on power struggles. When called upon, he would make helpful suggestions and would spontaneously offer up insights Isa would never have expected. But somehow the lemon vine was different for him. Not defeat, but it had ungrounded his energy. He hadn't been able to concentrate. Was he afraid of what they might create? Of what it might mean to the future? Or was he tired? Cedric was an old wizard, but his spells were starting to fail. His heart was listening to those who were questioning their motives and the morality of their manipulations. His heart could not keep pace anymore, not without being able to believe that what they were doing was truly right.

It was a Thursday when they first kissed. In a park. Not the kind with forests and wood chip trails, but the kind with paved paths and a man-made lake lined with groomed trees and plants designed to be at perfectly contrasting heights. Isa cited the genus and species for several, explaining their function in the interdependent web until David pulled her to a stop by the duck pond, took her in his arms, and kissed her.

His body was warm and his arms held her firmly. Isa melted against him. It was unexpected and wonderful. He was the perfect height. Every word and name and question and hypothesis escaped her head as her animal instincts took over. Gently, she led him back to the Oxford Arms. They kissed more on the way, they kissed intensely outside the main doors, but still they stayed outside. He glanced upstairs and smiled inquisitively.

Then it hit.

"You can't," Isa said. "I'm sorry. Goodnight."

"Oh. I.. are you sure?"

"No. Yes. We have to talk. We will talk about this later. There is something about me that you don't currently know and will need to know before you go through that door. Something you might not understand, or accept. I didn't want to tell you, because I like you. I really like you. I'm sorry it has come to this."

"What is it, Isa? What could be so bad? Are you sick?"

Instead of moving away as he asked, David inched closer and took her in his arms.

"You don't understand," she said, her eyes filling with tears. It was time. This would be the conclusion of the experiment. This piece of information was the one thing she never mentioned but suspected everyone knew. The thing she struggled every day to forget. "I used to be a man."

The geeks were always finding ways to improve the art of war. The instant a new gun is even rumored to come out, one of them pre-buys it and, when it finally arrives, has military dominance for a short while. Whoever did not have the military advantage had to watch their backs, always have a weapon at hand. Mr. Speed was definitely behind, and he'd wanted to buy the Gatling, but G-Man got to it first, and as per the rules of office warfare, no one could have the same weapon. This was true also for Mr. Speed's Annihilator XXI, which could shoot across the office, around the corner and pelt the bathroom doors. The aim was terrible, but by now everyone on the ninth floor was accustomed to having something whiz past.

Doreen didn't get the next three jobs, either. Would it be the food fair next? Wearing a costume and waving at cars out front a family restaurant chain? Panhandling? She wanted to hash it out with Isa, get it off her chest, but it wasn't the time. Isa had herself to deal with. Doreen had seen it before. She remembered the bald guy Isa had tried to date a couple years back. Failure. Depression plagued her for weeks. This one had been far better looking. Doreen would give her one more day, and then start pulling her back. Step one was the latte. Step two, a desert of some kind, something irresistible, and then sitting with her as she ate and talking about it a little but quickly moving on to less serious topics, such as the recreation of life. The day after would be Café Literal, if Isa was ready, and then it would be life as almost usual. She would be down. Truly bouncing back would take a while. Doreen could relate.

Now and then people got hit. Except Cedric. When they missed him most in the lab, the Geeks built up the legend of Cedric's anti-dart field. It never failed. It had been such a marvel that on the rarest occasions, one of the geeks would intentionally send one whizzing towards his feet. Whether his back was turned or not, each and every time they dart would curve away at the last moment or Cedric would happen to shift out of range. He'd never jump or jolt. But he might turn, nod at Mr. Speed or whomever, and smile. He would not be a casualty of this war. His battles were far more deeply entrenched.

The weekend came and went and still no word from the blue streak. He'd come and gone without a glance back. Doreen had succeeded in prying Isa out of her cramped apartment on a Saturday night to do something new. There was a bar downtown neither had been to, that was getting rave reviews: the Filibuster. Years before, it had been a funeral home. The embalming equipment was supposedly still in the basement. With the new capsule system of processing bodies, the home had gone out of business and sat dormant for years. Then, suddenly the Filibuster opened and was instantly hot. And that was where Doreen ordered them gin and tonics and began a discussion about how unfair love was, until she noticed the live music.

"Hey, it's Seven."

"What?"

"The kid from the second floor. You know, with the angry tabby. No wonder this place is so busy, that's his band, Seven and two halves."

Seven was on a small stage with his guitar, another man with a stand up bass, and a drummer, whose snare drum, bass, high hat, and single lone cymbal looked ancient and tiny. Seven was singing softly into his headset. They were playing something old and marvelous, a song by Gilberto Gil. Isa was impressed that Doreen knew who wrote it. Was there a secret studious side to Doreen?

They didn't feel a need to talk anymore, but let their thoughts wash away on the poetry of sound. Seven didn't recognize them when they left. He hadn't noticed them at all.

Seven was an odd little guy. He was the genetic evolution of a musician, and his popularity was growing. The girls flocked to him but he was shy and didn't know what to say or do. He played up his act through a shiny blue suit and slicked back hair, but deep down there were some insecurities that the casual onlooker would miss. As it turned out, he was quiet. And so he stared ahead, even when Doreen waved. She looked where he was looking, at the dark far corner of the room, but she saw nothing as she stepped out the door. She didn't see the lovely Japanese girl who was also looking back at Seven, realizing he had been singing to her for years and she hadn't known a thing until now.

Another week, no phone call. Isa wept too much. This summarized all the things her choice had cost her in life. All of it rolled into one massive rejection. Nepeta did her best to comfort her as Isa stayed home from the lab, curled up with tragic romance films and takeout menus. Now and then Doreen would drop off a latte and a quick hug, but it didn't help. Isa had been here before, but it was the knowledge that she would be here again that hurt the most.

Finally on Sunday she got the message on her answering machine. So he was a nice guy. Most would never shown their faces again. Maybe they would move neighborhoods to escape her. David wanted to meet tomorrow after work. A Monday. The worst possible sign. Isa knew it was pointless, but he wanted to prove that he was a nice guy, and talk to her in person, but she had seen the look on his face. It was like he'd swallowed a spider, and it was still wriggling around inside of him. He was disgusted. He was lost in a foreign city and didn't understanding the street signs, with landmarks to guide him.

Monday at Café Literal. 6:45 p.m. The chubby man strolled behind his small Mexican dog. Hefe smelled the air and following some indiscernible track. The man looked better, like the walks were doing him well. He still had the cane, but there was something lighter about his step. Still, he took his time, watched the trees – incredibly patient with the dog. They were best friends. They needed each other, this small shaky animal and lumbering giant of a man. They were opposites that had found a magnetic connection. They were damn lucky.

Isa sat alone. Doreen was having a job interview at a bakery. She'd gotten the call that morning. She said she would come by the apartment and describe the carnage in detail to Isa, later, after David was finished explaining himself. After it was over.

But David didn't come in sheepishly with an embarrassed look on his face. He came in like he always did, sleek, quick, his PVC jacket shining under Café Literal's dim lights.

"How've you been?" he asked, popping into the next chair. The question seemed almost rhetorical, because Isa hadn't put on makeup or done her hair in weeks. She was wearing a sweater and jeans, not date clothing. This wasn't a date. This called for comfort clothing.

David waited a while. Isa sipped her tea.

"I'm so sorry. I had to think about it a lot. I wasn't expecting it, and maybe I should have been. I should have been able to tell somehow. And I don't know. Was that insulting? This is… it's really new for me."

"I get it," she said. But then he was there, standing. His hands taking hers, guiding her upwards. He looked into her eyes, and there was something there. A spark of mischief.

"Yeah, sure, you get everything that has to do with biology. Why don't you show me your apartment," he said, "and I'll see for myself what mysteries you can show me." And with that he leaned forward and kissed Isa tenderly.

And the night from that moment on was perfect. On the second floor a Japanese woman shuddered with the careful touch of her seven-fingered lover. Across town an old scientist opened his eyes and saw his wife's face filled with relief and renewed joy. Downtown Doreen switched her footwork at incredible speeds as she punched a giant wad of rising dough back into its bowl. In his basement suit, the G-Man practice-loaded a ten shot foamy-dart gun. And at Usuteshihu, in the volatile, acidic, impossible soup that is the atmosphere of the planet Venus, the tiniest silver tendril was reaching into the darkness, searching against all odds for the optimum place to take root.

Brad Glenn is a writer, artist, and teacher in Edmonton, Alberta. He graduated from the University of Victoria from the department of writing, and has been writing fiction and poetry for the last thirty years. After Momma Died Carrying the Jelly Baby,  which is included in this book of short stories, was an award winner at the BC Festival of the Arts. In the last ten year Brad has been focusing his creativity creating comics and scripts, and has published a number of series.

CPSIA information can be obtained at www.ICGtesting.com
Printed in the USA
LVOW08s0840300716

498405LV00002B/3/P